Quiet Strength

BOOK I

Love's Mission

D1519693

Tina Hawkey Baker

DEDICATION

To the wonderful men in my life…

My husband, Robert

My dad, Jim Hawkey

My stepdad, Daniel Wolfe

You each have shown me that it is not in words alone that love is given, but those quiet precious moments where no words were spoken and you were there for me.

To my young men, Aaron, James and Timothy

You each possess the strengths of Ryan in your heart and body. I believe in each of you and can't wait to see God's promises fulfilled in your lives.

Acknowledgements

Special thanks

Chuck and Diane Hammond; you are my hope for the book cover on Quiet Strength, Book II. You are a truly beautiful couple inside and out. The love you two share is mirrored in the characters of Ryan and Amy. To love, to share to protect a marriage of commitment takes two, you lead by example not only to your eight children, but to those who look up to you and your faith in God.

Scott Hammond, tag you are it! You look the most like your dad and I appreciate you standing in as him for the book cover. Scott, you are a good young man. God has a great work for you.

Vanessa Hopwood, I have never met you. Diane adores you and speaks so kindly of your character and faith. I am writing this before I have even seen you to do the book cover. Diane told me that you could absolutely pass as her (we won't say how many years ago). I know you must be beautiful. Thank you for stepping in and helping out.

Judy Meier, without missionaries like you who are willing to sacrifice all for Christ, the progression of Christianity would be so much harder. You are an extraordinary example of Christ alive and well.

Mike Palmer, for giving me some of your valuable time and knowledge.

Robert Baker (my hub) and Francis Cooper for correcting me.

Thank you Lord and Savior, this is my offering

CONTENTS

CHAPTER ONE

SOMEONE CARES

Ryan didn't put a lot of thought into girlfriends, much less marriage. He wasn't your average high school graduate. His passion for Christ had driven him and kept him strong and focused since the first day he was handed a Bible and a hammer. He was a sophomore in high school at that time, and unemotional about everything, especially his future. He wasn't a trouble maker or an honor student. He looked like all the other teenage boys; he blended in with… no one. He stood in the crowd, but didn't belong. He existed, so neutral that he was never asked to join in or told to go away. It was 1966 and the free-love and flower-child era was coming into bloom. His parents worked to avoid being home and stayed out at night enjoying what they thought was freedom, leaving Ryan to raise himself.

It was a beautiful day in March. Most kids were excited about spring break. Where they were going and who was going with them controlled their thoughts and conversations. After spring break, it was a straight-forward countdown to high school graduation for the seniors and summer vacation for everyone else. College was the biggest challenge for most.

With the war raging on in Vietnam, a much talked about draft would take any young man without a plan. Ryan often thought about the war. He had nowhere to go; he would surely be drafted and sent to fight for his country. Whenever he thought about going to war, it wasn't being shot at or even dying for his country that saddened him. It was the thought of dying for his country and no one knowing, because as far as he could tell, no one knew he existed anyway. He had two more years before he was old enough to serve. He would sign up now and get dying over with if he could.

Ryan walked home with his hands in his front jean pockets and his head down. The sound of a vacuum cleaner caught his attention. A middle-aged man was cleaning out his 54 Chevy Bel-Air. It was two-tone with a white roof and powder-blue body. The car was nothing spectacular in the eyes of true "motor heads" who looked for dual-quad carbureted large V-8 engines with Positrac rear-ends and Firestone tires. But, it was well kept and shiny from the wax job it had just received, which is what caught Ryan's attention.

When the man looked up, he made eye contact with Ryan, causing him to stutter out a weak, "Hello," feeling the need to speak because he was caught staring. "Nice car, Sir," Ryan said as he continued walking.

"It's going up for sale tomorrow. You interested?" The man wrapped the cord of the vacuum around his arm and then shoved it through the handle.

"Even if I were interested, I couldn't afford the car." Ryan stopped as the man put the vacuum down and walked toward him.

"My name is Ed. It's nice to meet you." He held out his hand and waited for the awkward Ryan to shake his hand and tell him his name. Ed recognized the boy. He had seen him walking alone many times with the same posture. Several times he was driving and had seen Ryan unlock the door of a rundown duplex a couple blocks away. Ed's heart was stirred as he looked into the empty eyes of the boy.

Ryan weakly shook Ed's hand, he stood there not knowing if he should walk on or stay.

"You got a name?" Ed patiently waited for him to answer.

"Ryan, Ryan Nelson is my name, Sir," he replied.

"Come on over here Ryan and take a look at her." Ed was friendly and guided Ryan over to the car and popped open the hood. "I think I heard some whining in the engine when I drove her yesterday. Why don't you hop inside and start her up so I can watch the belts? The keys are in the ignition."

Ryan wanted to so badly. He had never sat in the driver's seat of a car much less started one up. He looked at the dashboard for a few moments. "Um, I don't know how," Ryan finally confessed while Ed was staring at the engine and waiting on him.

Ed was an upbeat and truly patient man. He had three girls under the age of seven, so the chance to do "guy" things was a fun change for him. He gave Ryan simple instructions and spoke to him as if they were partners doing a project together. "How can a man who just met me give me such a responsibility? I hope I don't start the car up and run over him!" Ryan turned the key and the engine started cranking.

"Go ahead and push on the gas pedal, just a little," Ed instructed.

With that, the engine started right up. Ryan's thoughts were running faster than the car's idle.

A few moments later, Ed called for Ryan to shut off the car and come to him. The two guys huddled over the engine. Ed explained a few simple mechanics to Ryan. Then he asked him to hand him the two wrenches on the bench and hold back the air cleaner housing while he tightened the loose alternator belt.

"That's it, all done. Go ahead and start her up again. Good! Now she is purring. OK, you can turn her off now." Ed shut the hood and grabbed a stained t-shirt to wipe his hands.

Ryan was amused at the way Ed referred to the car as "she." His reference gave the car personality and a sense of belonging.

"Thanks for your help, Ryan. You came in real handy today." Ed patted him on the back and laughed at him for having a smudge of oil across his cheek. "You are starting to look like a mechanic already!"

Ryan genuinely smiled, he felt so good. Having interaction with someone who took the time to teach him made Ryan feel special. As he turned to leave, a woman's voice bellowed from the front door of the house.

"Time to eat," she said, wiping her hands on her apron. "You two ready for dinner?" Ed's wife had been watching them from the front window.

She too recognized the boy and knew of his parents. Since they lived in a small Kentucky town, everyone knew everyone in one way or another. By fact or fiction, gossip was alive and well. Sometimes truth is worse than gossip, as was Ryan's case.

Ryan didn't know what to do. She was looking straight at him. "Don't just stand there young man. These girls are hungry and if you don't get in here and get cleaned up they will drag you in here themselves. I am not letting Ed make you work and not at least feed you!" She was not going to take 'No' for an answer.

Ryan washed his hands in the tidy half bath on the main floor of the two-story. When he came out, he was surprised to see everyone sitting at the table. "Come on over here and have a seat," Ed said, pulling the chair next to him out. "Ryan, this is my wife, Nancy, and my girls, Amanda, Becky, and Carol."

Ryan waved gently. The food smelled great and he was hungry. The girls held hands, Ed and Nancy followed. "Ryan, we give thanks to the good Lord before we eat. Bow your head please."

Eating together, praying together, and talking about their day were all more than Ryan could take in at once. He ate politely, even though he wanted to pick up the bowl and gulp down every drop of the vegetable soup. The bread melted in his mouth it was homemade along with the strawberry preserves he slathered on top. "So this is family," he thought to himself.

After dinner, Ryan and Ed went into the living room. Before they had a chance to sit down, all three girls came running with their arms full of books.

It was the best night of Ryan's life.

"Sorry, guy. It's time to be daddy to my angels. Reading, baths and bedtime, it's our routine." Ed walked Ryan to the door. He thanked Ryan for his help and Ryan in return thanked him for dinner. "I get home from work about four tomorrow. Do you want to stop by again?" Ryan's quietness mirrored his feelings. He thought it was a way of protecting himself. If he didn't say much, his voice wouldn't reveal how sad he really was to leave.

"If I can, I will." Ryan left without a handshake. He wished the night didn't have to end.

After the girls were bathed and put to bed, Ed and Nancy sat on the front porch with their coffee to watch the moon shine and the stars glimmer. "Are you thinking what I am thinking?" They didn't look at one another. Their hearts were heavy and their thoughts were deep. "Did you hear what I asked, Ed?"

"Yes, I heard you." Ed put his coffee cup down and pulled Nancy close to him, holding her while rubbing her shoulder. "He has been put in our lives for a reason." They talked for hours and prayed before going to bed themselves. They were going on a mission to make a difference in a young man's life and they didn't have to leave their yard to do it.

Chapter Two

A Bible and a Hammer

Ryan made it a point to be passing Ed's house at 4:15 p.m. the next day. He stopped and talked with Ed more. "Ryan, do you have plans for spring break?"

"No Sir, I don't have plans." Ryan was embarrassed at how free he was. He was completely free to come and go as he pleased. He had the life that his friends begged for, but Ryan hated it.

"Well, if you have time, I would love to offer you a job." Ed was serious. Ryan's heart flew to his throat.

"What?" Ryan spoke up in disbelief.

"We need some help putting a roof on the sanctuary at church. We are in desperate need for a new roof this spring and this summer we will be putting a new addition on the fellowship hall to add classrooms. We need good strong laborers. What do you think?"

Ryan just stood there, dumbfounded.

"I forgot to tell you that you won't have to worry about what you are doing with your money because it is free labor," Ed laughed.

Ryan wasn't thinking about the money. He was thinking

about having more time with Ed and his family. He was drawn to them for reasons he couldn't explain.

"I can do that," Ryan said assuredly.

"Are you sure? It's a big commitment. You will be lifting heavy building materials, working in the unpredictable spring weather and in the summer's heat. There will be times that you will go to work at sunrise and not get home until dark." Ed was really pushing Ryan for a commitment that he could remind Ryan of if he got discouraged.

"You can trust me Ed; I will be there for you." Ryan was as sure as anything that he wanted to be a part of whatever Ed was doing.

"Okay then, we have a gentleman's agreement. If you work well on the roof, we will bring you back in a few weeks to start helping on the addition. It will be an all summer job. Several men, including myself will be using their vacation time to help work. There will be a different work crew there every week. We need someone constant who knows what has been going on to keep everyone informed." Ed knew the pastor and Himself would be in charge. He wasn't lying to the boy. He was giving this young man hope and purpose.

"If this works out, to show my appreciation, I will give you Tess." Ed was dead serious about Tess, but Ryan was clueless who Tess was.

"Tess? Who is Tess?" Ryan's question and expression made Ed laugh so hard that tears trickled down his face.

"Sorry Ryan. Tess is the 54 Chevy I was going to sell. I have called her Tess since the day I drove her off the lot."

Ryan shook his head. "Really, a car?" He could not understand why a man he just met twenty-four hours earlier would be so kind to him.

That was the beginning of a life of meaning, need, and importance for Ryan. He had purpose every morning when he got up. He was always the first one there to meet whoever was available to work at the church. One day it might be a roofer he was with, the next day a plumber and then another day a drywall man who wanted to give estimates or take measurements. Ryan became the only constant figure on the job. Ed met him every morning at 7:00 a.m. The first thing they did was pray about the day and for safety. The second thing they did was read scripture from the Bible. After a week on the roof, Ed, the pastor, and every other worker who had been on the job trusted Ryan to do what they asked.

Later that week, there was an early-morning Friday meeting for the workers. It poured the rain, squelching any hopes of work for the day, so after the meeting, Pastor, Ed and Ryan went out to breakfast.

"You are doing a great job, young man." Pastor was such a great encourager. He built Ryan up and told him of his true value to God himself. As they sat in the booth, they had a deeper discussion about God's love and purpose for everyone's life. Ryan asked questions and his very soul soaked up every answer given about God's mercy and calling. After breakfast, Ryan prayed a sinner's prayer and became part of the biggest family he ever knew.

Ed laid a box that he had been carrying with him down on the table. "These are for you, Ryan." Ed pushed the box toward Ryan.

Ryan was overwhelmed with emotion. Every day he strived to show no emotion or the emptiness that tormented him. Now wasn't the time to hide. He was open and crying for the first time he could remember. He opened the box to find two objects. One was a beautiful black leather Bible and the other was a nice 20 oz. hammer. "Both of these gifts can help you to build your life and career." The Pastor hugged Ryan and welcomed him into the family of God.

The summer of 66 was an amazing transformation for Ryan. He changed mentally, physically and spiritually. The boy Ed met in March was no longer. Ryan learned to use a hammer and the Bible as a way of life. Physically, the skinny boy had gained twenty pounds of muscle. He filled his t-shirts out with ease and had to go up a pants size.

School was to start in a week. Ryan tried not to think about it. It wasn't that he didn't like school; it was that he had found a peace where he was and didn't want to change. The only change he was looking forward to was his school schedule. Carpentry, blueprint reading, plumbing, and heating, anything that had to do with building and repairing was what he wanted to do when he graduated. Ed had helped him to find his niche and his passion. The last Friday of summer break, Ed met Ryan at the church. He had the keys and the title of the 54 Chevy with him, just as he had promised.

CHAPTER THREE

AMY'S CHOICE

Amy Waltz was from a big family. She had two brothers, a sister, and more cousins then she could count. She had a love of children that started in her own childhood. She took immaculate care of her dolls and their accessories. She wanted to get married and have children as soon as possible, after graduation that was. She may have been only a high school junior, but she knew what she wanted. Amy loved her family life. Her dad owned a packaging company and was a strong man of God. Everything he did he prayed about. He took the Bible as his instruction book. He was good to people and he loved his wife and family.

Amy's mom was amazing. She made everything from scratch, sewed, knitted, and had the most understanding heart. She was a friend to many and a mom to more than her own children. Their house was the one that everyone wanted to come to. There was laughter, love, and prayer for all who came into their house.

Growing up in such a loving household kept Amy secure in who she was in God. She was treated as a person of value and that's how she chose to treat others. She was different than most girls. Being beautiful inside and out, Amy had what seemed like hundreds of friends and plenty of guys interested in her. The timing wasn't right for a relationship though, and Amy didn't play games or participate in the dating scene just to be dating. She loved learning new things and sharing all her knowledge with her mom and younger sister. They listened patiently and laughed at Amy's excitement over subjects that were way too hard for them to comprehend. Amy was smart, energetic, and enthusiastic. Teaching would be the perfect profession for her to get into.

Her junior and senior year flew by and choosing the right college was her most difficult task. Should she attend a local college or go out of state? She prayed for direction. Teaching became her goal, but finding the right person to share her life with was still her dream. After she had graduated the only thing stopping her from marriage was knowing who God had planned for her. She asked God to keep him safe and to stir passion daily in his heart, whoever he was. Amy had high standards for a future husband. He must love God first and her a very close second!

The spring and summer were full of revivals. Every month for at least a week, an evangelist would come and conduct nightly services at church. They were all good speakers and they all ministered to the congregation, challenging them all in their relationships with God. However, it was one man, a very humble dark skinned, gentle soul who captured Amy's attention the most. His name was Bill and he was there to talk about Maldives. Amy had never heard of Maldives before. It took her ten minutes to find the island nation in the Indian Ocean on the globe.

Bill explained all these details and brought to life this small nation in Asia. He showed slides of the villages and the beautiful islands and beaches. The faces of the children captured Amy's heart. They were in such need of housing, education and of course, God. This man had a deeper passion for others then she had ever known. He was leaving on the first of July to go back for a month. He talked about the changes going on in Maldives with the Governments push to enforce its Islamic roots. Britain had protected Maldives until 1965 when an agreement was signed ending their responsibility. The window to reach out to the islanders for Christ's sake was closing. Christianity was already forbidden. "Even unto death," Bill said with tears streaming down his face. "We must do all we can to reach them with the gospel."

Amy was heartbroken, and she became determined to help. As soon as service was over she spoke with Bill. Her heart pounded and her body felt feverish with emotion. She was being called by God to join Bill. Now she had to convince her dad that it was the right thing for her.

When they got home and settled in for the night, Amy approached her dad, careful not to overwhelm him with all her information and reasoning. Her dad listened and never commented. Amy thought his silence was a hint that things weren't going her direction. "Well Dad, say something.'" Amy couldn't take the suspense of what her dad was thinking any longer.

"Amy, I saw you talking with Bill. I saw the look in your eyes and knew what was happening." He walked toward Amy smiling. "You know I have seen that look in your eyes before." He knew his daughter well. "I will support you. However, when you return from your trip, you will have to live at home and attend the local college." Mr. Waltz said everything Amy needed and wanted to hear. He was giving her permission and financing her. His conditions were reasonable.

"I can do that Dad and thank you!" Amy hugged her dad so tightly that he gasped for air.

Amy was so excited and could hardly wait to tell Bill. At church that Sunday night, Amy explained how she felt lead to go with him.

He was as excited for her as he was for himself. He gave Amy a contact number and got her address. "You will receive all the information next week. I will meet you at the Cincinnati airport with whoever else feels led to come. Pray Amy," he sounded so serious. "There is opposition everywhere. The war, government, and finances, so much that God has to work out. We need strong volunteers. There is one more thing Amy..."

His words pierced her soul and tears filled her eyes.

He went on, "You cannot bring one thing; absolutely nothing religious. No Bibles, crosses, hymnals, nothing at all. They do not have religious freedom in Maldives. You will be severely punished or worse if you are caught." Bill was giving Amy an honest view of evil, but did not want to make her think there was no hope. He cleared his throat, and softened his tone as he continued, "If you gain the trust of the mothers, you will have children all over you. They will love you and follow you everywhere. They are so hungry for hope. Your job will be to gain their trust and keep them busy and safe as we work."

He gave a half smile and continued on to search for the pastor. He had to give the gravest of details and warnings to protect her and everyone else on the trip. He was leaving that night to find another church to give his testimony. He had four months of traveling ahead of him. He wanted to take the best of everything back to the islanders that he had fallen so deeply in love with.

CHAPTER FOUR

CLOSED WINDOWS TO AN OPEN DOOR

Two weekends after visiting Amy's church, Bill found himself in a pretty little town over the border of Kentucky. A country church south of town caught his eye. It had been remodeled with a large addition of sided exterior walls attached to the original brick building. All evidence of construction was gone with the exception of a neatly stacked pile of 2x4's in the back parking lot. The landscaping was perfect with not one sign of trash or weeds anywhere. "Someone really cares about this church," he said to himself. He heard a soft voice that he had heard so many times before, telling him to go up and knock on the door. It was a Friday night and Bill thought it strange to knock at a church door on a Friday night, but did as he felt led. When no one answered, he turned to leave.

"Can I help you?" asked a man who had just pulled up with a car full of kids.

"My name is Bill Alden, and I am representing the country of Maldives. I am sharing my testimony and need with God's people for an outreach. I have pictures, slides, brochures, and whatever you would need to validate my sincerity."

15

"We are here to open up the church for a youth gathering tonight. Wait here a minute and I will be right back." Ed parked the car. "I will call the pastor. Maybe he could come and talk to you." As soon as Ed had stopped the car, the girls had thrown open the back doors and were running all around the church.

"Amanda, Becky, and Carol, stay away from the building materials!" Ed hollered out to the girls. "I'll be right back. This young man here is Ryan," pointing to Ryan as he got out of the passenger's side. "Why don't you two chat while I go inside?" Ed looked through his keys before finding the right one for the church.

Bill and Ryan sat on the sidewalk and watched the girls run around so freely. Bill wished every child had the ability to run and play as they did. They were carefree, healthy, and obviously loved. Ryan was curious about the man. He wasn't familiar with missionaries.

"Where are you from?" Ryan asked to start up a conversation.

"Originally Michigan," replied Bill. "I have been working in Maldives for two years though. My contract just ended there last year. I know my work isn't done there." Bill looked down at his feet and kicked at a rock. "These people live on next to nothing. They do not have proper medical attention or education. There are over 1,000 coral islands that make up Maldives. The biggest island is their capital, Malé. It's only a little over nine miles long and two miles across. The country is so small that half the world doesn't know it exists." Bill leaned back and put his arms behind him to prop him up. "I am sorry. I just can't get them out of my mind. I don't mean to ramble on, but I know I do."

"It's okay. I can tell you care a lot for these people." Ryan had been listening with more than his ears. He too heard the heart of a man who was burdened for the islanders. He

16

couldn't imagine caring so much for strangers that you give up your life and freedom for them.

The pastor came to meet Bill at the church. The youth were being very noisy, but having a lot of fun. Ryan stayed with Bill as he spoke to the pastor. He focused on every situation and on every need that Bill shared with the pastor. The pastor agreed to have Bill speak to the congregation on Sunday morning.

"Where are you staying?" Ryan asked out of curiosity and desire to hear more from Bill.

"Point me in a direction young man. I haven't checked in anywhere and it's getting pretty late. Do you know a good hotel in town? Bill yawned and stretched. He was ready for a good night sleep.

"Sure I do, it's cheap too!" Ryan was excited with his offer. It was Friday. His parents hadn't been home for a weekend in almost two years unless it happened to be a holiday. "You can stay at my house, I'll sleep on the couch, and you can have my room."

Any other time Bill would insist on staying at a hotel, but he was so tired and Ryan was so genuine that he couldn't resist, "Sure, okay for tonight anyway."

It wasn't at all the restful night that Bill had in mind. Ryan had him up half the night asking questions and talking about Maldives. Bill was very candid about the dangers in Maldives. Bill explained to Ryan the disguise they would be using to go back to the island. They were going to build a large community building for gatherings, doctor visits, teachers, and etc. They would mainly be working and loving these sweet people who didn't have a clue what bondage they were in. However, whenever it was safe, they would do a "special" work for God. Ryan was so excited about the thought of "special" work in Maldives that he couldn't sleep. He finally got the hint it was time for bed when Bill fell asleep mid-sentence. While

17

Ryan lay awake on the couch he prayed and asked God if there was any way for him to travel with Bill that he would please let it happen.

All day Saturday and into the night Ed, Ryan and Bill walked around town and talked with different businesses about sponsoring Bill's trip. Ryan had shared his desire to go with Bill to everyone he talked to. He truly was over the top excited about the possibility of going to Maldives. Some gave donations and some made promises to donate when the time got closer. People couldn't resist or deny the young man's enthusiasm or Bill's passion. They made a good team. Ed was amazed at the giving and promised Ryan that what he didn't raise, he would sponsor the difference. He had only two things in his way, the war, and the need for a passport.

As he left that night to continue to share his heart and mission, Bill made himself visible for those whom God had already chosen for His team, even though His team may not have known that they were 'the chosen'. When they would hear God say "GO!" they would all be packing their bags for Maldives within weeks.

April 2nd marked the eighteenth birthday of young Mr. Ryan Nelson. It was a happy day for him; his parents actually remembered and were home to spend the day with him. The church had decided to throw a surprise party for him the Friday following his birthday. He had worked hard for the church and it didn't go unnoticed. Not only was he a huge help with the roof and addition, he had taken over all the landscaping and maintenance for the church. He was well loved and appreciated. The church shocked him with an abundance of cards each containing some form of money. They wanted to bless his efforts in coming up with the money for a passport and airplane ticket. The congregation gave a whopping $458.67. The board members voted to make up the difference of $41.33 for a total of $500.00! Ryan laughed and cried. He felt more love and appreciation on this day than he ever had before. Monday would be a big day for him. He would apply for a passport and register for the draft.

Two weeks passed, three weeks passed. Ryan kept a 2:00 vigil on the mail box at home. Where ever he was at around two, he made it a point to stop by his house and check the mail. Four weeks and two days after applying for his passport, a special envelope with Ryan's name on the front awaited him; it wasn't the document he wanted. It read, "Order to Report for Armed Forces Physical Examination 7:00 in the morning at the Federal Building." Ryan didn't understand. He thought for sure that God was leading him to the mission field and college. It was Wednesday and the date on the paper was for the following Monday. Ryan had seen this before. His classmates were going in for their physicals and the following week, being shipped off to boot camp. Some things didn't seem fair. All he could do was pray and ask others to pray for God's will. Ryan wasn't afraid to serve his country. He would do so proudly, but he had this aching feeling that he was supposed to do something different.

Monday morning at 6:45 Ryan climbed the stairs of the Federal Building. When he opened the stairway door, he was surprised to see three other guys his age standing there waiting for the clock to turn to 7:00. They all had the same look of bewilderment and confusion. Their lives were not in their control. The Selective Service Department now had the say of where their lives were headed. A few more guys joined them in line and at 7:00 sharp the door opened and they were herded in to a room. Everything was done together. There wasn't any privacy or 'get to know you' conversation. They were strictly paperwork in motion. Standing in their underwear was embarrassing and cold. Height, weight, sight, hearing, blood pressure, lungs, and heart were checked in assembly line style.

"You are a 1-A son. You are a 1-A also. Move on" and

"Next!" were the only words being heard in the room.

Then it was Ryan's turn. He went in every direction they asked, but instead of being told to move on, they asked him to stand against the far wall of the room. Six more guys were ushered through with the same, move on and next demands. Ryan was the last man standing. He was called back to the line to stand and wait for instructions. This time, two doctors with stethoscopes appeared. They both listened to Ryan's chest, asking him to breathe in and out. Stepping back from Ryan, both doctors agreed and explained to him. "You are a 4-F young man. You have a heart murmur and are unable to serve your country." As quick as that, Ryan was dismissed. He walked out, feeling both relieved and saddened. While he was spared, he knew others were not.

It was all a waiting game now. With only five weeks left before Bill left for Maldives, there was still no sign of a passport. Ryan did not know how to feel. Not that he had wanted to be drafted, but it was what he expected. His hope was to do the mission trip above all, yet nothing was falling into place. Ryan worked hard doing what he could for whomever he could. He learned so much from Ed and the men at church. He had become very handy with a variety of machines and tools. Every penny he could spare above his tithe and food, he saved for the possibility of going with Bill.

With choices waning, Ryan signed up for college. He wanted to do an apprenticeship to better hone his skill and broaden his abilities. The closest college was the University of Cincinnati. When he went there, everything fell into place as if it were already planned out and waiting on him. They offered Ryan the apprenticeship and a room in the dorm. He had prayed, but still didn't expect any of the miracles that had just taken place. He had spent the first eighteen years of his life surviving; now he was living.

He was quiet as he drove home that afternoon. Usually

the radio would be blaring and he would be tapping the steering wheel to the beat, but not today. He meditated on what had happened at the university. This was the path his future was supposed to take. It was the right thing to do, he felt it strongly. Out of habit, as soon as Ryan got home, he checked the mail box. Sitting on top of the pile was a government envelope marked passport. Ryan smiled and looked to the sky. God knew how the events needed to happen. If the passport would have come first, Ryan would have never signed up for college. God had a plan and God had a purpose.

Working hard, saving money and getting everything settled before he left had consumed his time for the last month. Finally, the night before leaving for Maldives, Ryan sat down with Ed and Pastor and shared his heart and thankfulness that God brought them into his life. It didn't take a lot of words between them because Ed and Pastor had both sensed the need of this young man. They were happy to be an instrument of God. For two years they had prayed with, taught, and led Ryan to be a leader. Now was his time to take all he had learned and give it away.

CHAPTER FIVE

A LONG, LONG WAY

Bill stood at the front of the airport waiting. Four plus himself, he had hoped for many more volunteers. With one of the volunteers being a female, Bill wasn't sure if she was going to be more of a help or hindrance because she would need to be watched and protected.

It was hot in Maldives, tropically hot! This would be a new and trying experience for the four of them. Bill knew that they wouldn't be coming if they were not led to come. He had to trust God.

Twin brothers, Mark and Wayne from Fairfield, Ohio were the first to show up. They were skinny fellows that both looked and acted alike. The two of them together weighed as much as one mature man. They were very protective of their carry-on bags, although they freely left their other luggage lying on the floor for everyone to step over. Bill hoped they weren't going to be slobs because their hut had barely enough room to sleep and eat. Since Amy was with them, she would have the small curtained off area where he usually slept. They were going to be in very close quarters, and he didn't want to be having to dig his bed out from under their things every night.

Shortly afterward Ryan came and then Amy. Everyone was there. They said their good-byes to their family. Ed gave Ryan a big embrace of love and pride. "Go, son. Do well, bless the islanders and come back even stronger and wiser." Ryan was the only one with a tearful farewell. They others didn't understand the depth of what just happened. They didn't need to; it was a special moment between Ryan, Ed, and God.

A long day of flying was ahead of them. The first part of the trip was a short flight to New York. The second part was from New York to London which was a long seven-hour flight, but that wasn't the worst of it. After a four-hour layover in London, they changed planes once again for another 11-hour flight. Stopping to refuel the plane made the whole trip, from beginning to end, a full 24 hours. Maldives time was nine hours ahead of Ohio time. In a nut-shell, they were leaving Ohio at 9:00 in the morning of August 3rd and were arriving in Maldives at 6:00 in the evening on August 4th. They were all jet lagged by the time the plane landed in Maldives. There wasn't much conversation between the five of them on the plane. Since all their tickets were purchased separately, their seats were spread throughout the plane. Their initial bonding consisted of small talk between flights. The true getting to know each other would be as they worked together on the island.

Gamini, a dear friend of Bill's, met them at the airport. With his shining white teeth contrasting brightly against his dark skin, he beamed with excitement to see his friend. "So good you back. I miss you." The two men hugged like long-lost friends.

They walked over to customs expecting to pick up their luggage and be on their way, but that wasn't at all how things happened. Customs was a horrible experience for all of them. Amy's purse was dumped, not gently either. The customs workers seemed to have contempt for them. Their entire luggage was opened and searched thoroughly. The once neatly folded clothes were thrown back into the luggage in a heap. Mark had brought a history book to read on the airplane. It was confiscated because it had the word God in it several times. For instance, God's name is in the constitution, on our currency and other documents that America was founded on.

"That's my book," Mark exclaimed. "I want that back!"

"Mark, you have to stop!" Bill said through gritted teeth. "The more attention you draw to us the more problems we will have."

The guards motioned for the carry-on luggage that they all had with them. Amy's was simple. She had brought many spools of yarn to crochet little things for the children. Her bag was stuffed with bright colors of yarn. She was handed her things back and asked to step aside. Bill was next. He had a small bag that consisted of snacks, writing paper, drafting paper, pencils, pens and a calculator. He was passed through and he took a spot by Amy. Ryan was laughed at. He had a bunch of socks and underwear, one toothbrush and four tubes of toothpaste in his bag.

"I am a simple man. What can I say?" He was embarrassed that they pulled everything out, but he was quick to be moved on.

Mark and Wayne weren't so fortunate. Mark had made a scene and they were going to make him squirm for it. Mark got all excited and waved his hands to try to stop the guard from handling his things so roughly. Five different sizes of harmonicas, snacks, and underwear filled Mark's bag. "Be careful with those harmonicas, they are valuable," Mark begged. The guard paid no attention to his pleas and shoved them back into his bag.

Finally, it was Wayne's turn. "Can I empty them, please?" Wayne was trying to stress the value of the contents of his bag.

"There are two sets of bongos in the bags. You know, bongos." Wayne cupped his hands and pretended to play the bongos to demonstrate what they were. The guards looked at the small bongos. They were intrigued by the size.

"You play?" one of the guards asked and handed them to Wayne.

"Yes, they are mine." Wayne was thankful to have them in his hands again.

"YOU PLAY!" The guard was loud. It was then that Wayne understood that he wasn't getting asked a question; he was being told to play the bongos.

Bill gestured to Wayne to play. He mouthed the words, "Do as he asks." The atmosphere was tense.

Wayne sat down on the guard's chair and put the bongos between his knees, situating them perfectly. He closed his eyes for what seemed forever as the guards started to get impatient with him. Slowly and quietly Wayne started tapping the outside rim to the bongos. He started humming gently and bobbing his head to the beat he tapped out. Softly, Mark blew into the harmonica adding eeriness to the bongos. A few seconds later, Wayne picked up the beat and played faster and louder while still bobbing his head. Mark kept pace, drawing out in perfect pitch every chord. Travelers began to seek out the music and walk toward the area where they all waited. When the guards noticed the crowd gathering, they held up their hands for Mark and Wayne to stop the music. The guards seemed disappointed that the brothers really knew how to play. Ryan and Amy didn't understand what was going on. It was a mystery why they seemed targeted by the officials in customs.

The guard insisted on rushing them off. They were all cleared and freed to continue.

A sigh of relief overcame them, but no one said a word. Everyone gathered their suitcases and followed Gamini to the taxi. Ryan and Amy stacked the luggage strategically as the others navigated seating arrangements in the taxi. It was too big a challenge. They managed to squeeze in almost everything, but not everyone. Without question, they needed two taxis. Bill and Gamini never stopped talking. The brothers were taking pictures of any and everything, trying to put what had just happened in the back of their minds. Ryan and Amy climbed over a couple of large duffle bags and wiggled down into their seat. The two of them shared what should be space for one. A smaller taxi with the other four travelers lead the way for the loaded down taxi carrying Ryan, Amy, and the luggage. It was a short trip that took them to the dock where a boat awaited them.

"I am confused. Why are we here?" Wayne asked the question that they all wanted the answer to.

Gamini laughed and said accusingly, "You no tell young people everything Bill. Shame is on you!" They both smiled at the young adults and continued to chuckle. It was good to laugh after such a stressful event.

"Gamini, if I tell them everything, I would never get anyone to come here." Bill wiped his eyes as tears trickled from his laughter.

"Excuse me," Mark said, stepping up to the men. "You want to explain what's so funny?" Mark and Wayne seemed frustrated, but Ryan and Amy didn't care. They knew they had come too far to go back now, so whatever it was, they were ready.

"I am sorry," Bill said as he regained his composure. "We are only half way to our destination."

"What? Are you kidding me?" Now Wayne's anxiety level hit its peak.

Ryan walked between Wayne and Bill. He didn't like the sudden outbreak from Mark or Wayne and trusted Bill would explain if the brothers would calm down. "Aren't we in Maldives?" Wayne understood the positioning of Ryan; he

26

changed his tone and paused for Bill's explanation.

"Yes, we are in the country of Maldives. However, there are many islands in this country. We are going to the Fuvahmulah Island to the district of Dhadimago. It is roughly 300 miles from here. If weather is on our side, this boat should get us there in twenty four hours or so." Bill wasn't sure if the brothers were going to attack him after he gave them this information or not. He was very glad that Ryan was standing between them, just in case.

It wasn't until Mark and Wayne went back to the taxi and started unloading their luggage that he was certain they were going to stay. Getting the luggage settled on the boat and paying for both taxis took another half hour. It was now after 7:00. Gamini had food waiting for them. They had never tasted such fresh tropical fruit before. The coconut, mangos, and pineapples melted in their mouths. They had some fruits and vegetables like back home too. Tomatoes, cabbages, cucumbers, and carrots were all cut up and put in hollowed-out coconut shells used as bowls. The journey had started off rough, but they were all content now with their bellies full. The brothers had even apologized to Bill for their behavior. Bill understood the stress and accepted their apologies. He warned not only the brothers, but Amy and Ryan too, "Do not draw attention to yourself. If customs wants to, they can throw you right out of Maldives. They have strict orders not to allow troublemakers on the island. By the way," Bill paused for clarity, "they consider Christians troublemakers."

They piled their duffle bags up against the side of the boat and leaned back. It was then they noticed the beauty of the sunset shimmering across the waters. The water was so clear and reflective. Sea-life could be heard splashing at times, other than that, they all rested and basked in the artwork of God.

Chapter Six

History of a Passion

They all woke up as the temperature rose with the sunrise. Five barrels of fresh drinking water lined the one side of the boat and water for washing lined the other. Gamini breaded eggplant and browned it on a hot plate heated from a generator. It not only smelled delicious, but it tasted wonderful! Ryan had never even heard of eggplant before. Amy had heard of it, but had before never tried it because she didn't like the way it looked. It's funny how when you are hungry, all your past reasons for not trying something disappear.

After breakfast, they took turns cleaning themselves up the best they could. They helped to unfold the large canopy so they would have protection from the sun and still be able to see the beauty of the islands from the water. Bill and Gamini gathered the others. They needed to talk to them about the island they were going to. The five Americans had a lot to learn before they arrived.

Bill spoke first. He gave the history of Gamini and himself. There were so many things that fell into place. The "unusual" and the "that really should of never happened" and of course, the "what a coincidence" were constant throughout the story. However, looking back, it was God and Him working out His plan by using those willing to listen. He explained how Gamini got into construction work in Malé.

Gamini was eighteen when he traveled to Malé with his father. They had brought coir rope and woven mats to sell at the market in the city. As they were walking, they came upon a group of people standing at the bottom of a tall structure. The closer they got, the more they could hear the people discussing treatment for the young worker who had fallen off the makeshift scaffolding. He was disorientated yet trying to plead his case to his boss that he would be fine. No one believed him. His boss made a co-worker take him to the small building down the road. It was the closest thing to a hospital the country had. As the remaining construction workers huddled together to discuss the great difficulty they were going to have continuing on with the job, Gamini overheard something that caught his interest.

Speaking in their Dhivehi language, Gamini joined in the conversation. "I can climb this for you," Gamini said in a voice of promise and confidence. Gamini loved to climb. It was part of his DNA. All the boys in his village climbed. "I climb and do whatever you want. I work hard for you." The construction workers were in a bind and Gamini was very convincing.

"Go ahead and show us how fearless you are, young man." The boss stepped aside and pointed to the area three stories high. If Gamini wanted a job, he would need to prove his worthiness. Without effort, Gamini climbed the tall scaffolding, walked out on the support beam, and waved. The job was his.

Gamini quickly discovered how diverse the city could be. Americans had been asked to join in the building up and modernizing of the capital Malé. Often, Gamini found himself in a situation unable to understand what he was supposed to do. He was frustrated and feared he would lose his job. The perfect timing of God stepped in one day as Gamini took some blueprints over to the medical building. He heard the doctor speaking in English to an American who needed assistance removing a splinter from under his thumbnail. After the American left, Gamini went in and introduced himself to the doctor, whose name was Jameel.

He found out that Jameel had traveled to America in the late 1950's. He studied hard to become a doctor in preparation to practice in Malé. Gamini saw an opportunity that would benefit both Jameel and himself. In exchange for English lessons, Gamini would put in extra hours to do much needed repairs and updates. Jameel agreed to Gamini's offer. Through this, they become friends. Being bilingual was a big advantage to both of them.

Gamini would have breaks to visit his family in Fuvahmulah. He married Ari and fathered two children with her. They stayed in Fuvahmulah with the rest of his family and islanders while he worked on the main island. They loved to see Gamini come back from Malé. All the village children would run to him looking for surprises he would bring to them. Gamini was one of the lucky ones who had a job off the island. His job was a means of supplying, not only his family, but the islanders of basic needs and little something's to give the kids. The traveling was tough, but had become a way of life. Gamini was respected in his village and in Malé. He was a quick study and willing to do whatever he was asked. The traveling between the islands gave Gamini a lot of time to think. He didn't understand how he could be as lucky as to be able to work in Malé. It wasn't until he met Bill that he put the pieces of fate versus God's will in order.

Bill was an engineer for the United States of America who had been asked to help in the process of developing the island.

He prayed about this opportunity and the answer came easy. The people of Maldives were mysterious and little was known about their history. He didn't know why, but he did feel that God was calling him. He accepted the job and worked hard to establish relationships with the people he was working with in Malé. He spent months trying to break through and make contacts. In his heart, he knew he was supposed to be there. He didn't have any connections until he met Gamini.

Gamini was a sponge of sorts. He was everywhere and open to learning and trying new things. The instant Bill met him, he knew Gamini would be his connection. They became good friends and shared a lot about the customs of their homelands. Gamini was amazed at the stories of technology and freedoms. Gamini took Bill to Fuvahmulah to see his island and meet his people. Because Bill cared for his people, Gamini trusted him. Gradually Bill introduced his relationship with God to Gamini. At first he was being a friendly listener, but as Bill shared in love the freedom of having a relationship with God, he started longing for the same closeness with the God that Bill loved.

Bill's contract to the islands was for two years, from 1965 to1967. During those years, he fell in love with the islands and its people. They were close knit families that took care of each other. They had poor health care and lost many babies and mothers during childbirth. There were not any schools with chalkboards and books on many of the islands. They were decades behind in their education, medical successes and technology.

When Bill's contract work was completed, he promised Gamini he would find a way back. Saying good-bye was heartbreaking. Bill had helped birth a love between God and Gamini. He wanted to share so much more than his experience, he wanted to share God's word. There was one very major problem with his want. Maldives is one of only a

31

few countries in the world where only one faith can be practiced publicly. Maldives is the only nation which legally tells you that you must practice not only Islam, but the specific government version of Sunni Islam. Anyone not practicing the Islamic religion was considered a sinner and unable to own land, be a citizen or participate in any functions privileged to citizens. Anyone caught practicing or under the suspicion of practicing anything other than Islamic religion can be reported to the government and imprisoned for three to five years, deported, fined or can simply disappear. The cost was high.

Gamini knew the risk he was taking, but he agreed to the challenge. Therefore, with nothing more than trust in God, the two said good-bye believing that they would soon be reunited. Bill came to the island an engineer and would return a man on a mission.

When Bill arrived back to the States, he opened his own engineering company. Only doors that God had the power to open led the way. He had government clearance so he was allowed to bid on out of country contracts. He worked tirelessly on bids to design anything that had to do with Maldives. Any extra money he received, he put back for another trip to the islands. He hired two partners, who were made aware of his plans. Bill offered them steady work, but they had to keep the office running in his absence. The partners were Christians; they could plainly see Bill's passion for Maldives. It was so radiant his partners soon shared his vision. Bill spent the first four months of 1968 building his business. He under-bid every offer going to Maldives in order to secure a contract, the more he sacrificed for Maldives, the more successful his company became. It was that spring that Bill set out to find volunteers to go with him back to Maldives.

He prayed for hard working, loving and accepting people. They had to be willing to take some risks. God gave him Ryan, Amy, Mark, and Wayne. He thought there would be more willing to come with him, but Bill had to trust that God knew what He was doing.

When Gamini spoke, it was all to the point. "Maldives will soon be a Republic. We are not under the British monarchy anymore. My country is changing. Religion is the law. It is true, what you call radical religion. We have no freedoms of worship. We do as we are told or suffer according to the government interpretation of the Islam's law.

"We are going to Fuvahmulah. It is the closest island to the equator and the furthest from Malé. It is where I was born." Gamini paused, his face sullen. Everyone waited; they could feel the heaviness of Gamini's heart. "My island has been a hidden treasure. We have beauty beaches and pools of freshwater. We are poor, but self-sufficient. Soon, the Republic will be doing more to make Fuvahmulah accessible. They make promise of medical and education. They say change be good for us, but they no tell truth." Gamini's facial expression said as much as his words.

"They rumors, great talk of good life. I work in Malé and I hear so much talk all time. Recent I hear about the Island of Giraavaru. It is eleven km from airport. Governments force everyone from island. It is home to no one now. The island suffered erosion and had too many women for Islamic laws to be fulfilled. The Government say not enough men for Friday Islamic prayer. There is so much… I hear they bring large buildings onto island so foreigners visit. They are, um…" he struggled, trying to find the right English word.

"Hotels," Amy offered as a help.

"Yes, hotels they call them. All words are hush-hush to the islands. This will be a sad time for my people. I am afraid this will mean I will not see you more after this mission." Gamini's voice had changed. He was excited to see them at the airport, now he was solemn like he was already grieving their departure. He understood what changes were coming more than anyone, with the exception of Bill.

"I explain little to my people. They no know what evil truth is under promises of the Republic." He wiped the sweat from his forehead and paused as if trying to find a way to tell a secret. "Friends, I am marked. The Republic has eyes to me. My family and I are in future danger. Today at the airport, you have troubles because you with me and you Americans. Be careful. My God is only protection. A time comes when I deny Christ or die." His voice trailed off as the captain of the boat walked through the middle of their circle. It was noticeable to all of them how Gamini stopped his conversation. "My friends, I will never bow." He didn't need to say more. Since Gamini started a relationship with God, he has been under suspicion for not participating in Islamic prayer. He never denied Allah, but a time of confession was inevitable.

Mark and Wayne finally spoke up. Come to find out, they were very good actors. Mark spoke first, explaining how his father had been a missionary many years ago to China. Travel was hard there and the danger of being a Christian in China was just as dangerous then as it is now. Wayne added that Bill was a good friend of their dad and that is why they agreed to do this mission. "Our dad always said that one mission trip would open your eyes for a lifetime." Wayne looked around for the captain. He didn't see him at first, but when he spotted him at the stern of the boat, he drew everyone in close and whispered, "Dad said Mark and I have the important information."

"What is that?" asked Ryan.

"Shush, please, not a good time to talk," Bill whispered.

"We are carrying something illegal into another country. These people are being lied to and we do nothing!" Amy's frustration rang out even through gritted teeth. "Shouldn't you warn them?" Amy's concerned voice had carried further than she thought. The captain turned to see the commotion. Amy stood up to look over the boat's edge. Ryan stood up and came alongside her for support.

"This isn't fair, Ryan!" Amy trembled, partly in fear, partly in anger.

"I know Amy. But with the time we have here and now, let's do our best to love these people and give them hope." Amy's hand was white knuckled grabbing tightly to the rail. The waters were calm; it was her emotions that raged causing her to feel the need to hang on. Ryan gently reached over and put his hand on top of hers. His strong hand covered hers and for a moment he was able to comfort her troubled heart.

Gamini set the rules for the missionary group. There should be no talk of God until they reach his village. The people of the archipelago understood works. They were thrilled to have people of knowledge come to help them build facilities. The ministry of works is what the people accepted as love and favor. They were intelligent and eager to learn. "Work hard and they will respect you," were the words of wisdom from Gamini.

At 6:00 in the evening, exactly fifty-eight hours from the time they left Cincinnati's airport, they docked at Fuvahmulah. Awaiting them on the shore wasn't a nice air conditioned vehicle, but six bikes with big baskets attached to the back fender area. "Oh no, you are kidding me again, right?"

"Sure is Mark," chimed in Amy sarcastically.

"Don't panic Mark. It is only a twelve-hour bike ride from here." The brother's eyes grew as big as the pineapples they enjoyed earlier. Gamini could not keep a straight face and gave up Bill as a tease.

"No, no brothers, it only five hundred peddles to village. If you slow peddle it take an hour, if you peddle with desire, half that time." The brothers were gullible. Amy and Ryan tried not to laugh. They hadn't said so, but it was evident they wanted to remain neutral in the bantering.

Even though they were all tired from jet lag, the bike ride to the village seem to invigorate them physically, giving them back the energy they had lost sitting still for so long. There were no paved roads, only beaten down paths, which seemed only appropriate for the island.

CHAPTER SEVEN

MALDIVES THE BEAUTIFUL

The island was beautiful, so beautiful that words could not do it justice. The island was peaceful and primitive. It was quiet in the sense that there were no cars, lawn mowers, or radios but, in stillness the island had its own sounds, of the ocean, wildlife, and birds chattering amongst themselves. The language of the inhabitants was a distinctive form of the Dhivehi language known as Mulaku bas. It was so different from what they had ever heard that it too seemed like an unknown noise.

The villagers were welcoming and simple people. They were as beautiful as their island. Their skin was smooth and dark, their eyes so black you couldn't see their pupils and their smiles revealed the joy of their hearts. Ryan had never experienced such simplicity and lack of drama. It seemed to him that he was getting a glimpse of what heaven would be like. There was a variety of huts and bungalows scattered around the village. The hotel they would be staying at for the next month was a mud hut with a divider separating a small section in the back which would be Amy's room. A pallet of four beds lay in the larger room with two lanterns. A small table that stood about six inches off the ground was in the common room with another lantern sitting in the middle. There were no chairs anywhere. Once they put their luggage in the rooms, Gamini took them for a walk along the beach.

It was dusk now and the sunset was slipping over the ocean with its warm colors softly saying goodbye to another day. From the beginning, the brothers stayed together. They were so much alike. They laughed at things that no one else did as if they had a secret language and understanding of their own. Anyone could tell that they came from a strong and close knit family. Bill mingled sometimes, but mostly stood in silence alone, yet not alone. His demeanor seemed prayerful. He stood at the edge of the ocean with his eyes closed with such purpose; it was obvious he was standing in the presence of God. That left Ryan and Amy together. They noticed one another from the beginning. They were the same age with the same passion for helping people. They were drawn to each other in many ways, but they never forgot the reason they were on the island.

After a rather tough night's sleep, they were up at sunrise to labor before it got too hot. They had eggplant and fruit for breakfast, and then off to work. From 6:00 in the morning until high noon, they focused on the layout, design, and supply list for a large building. Gamini and Bill would make the long trip back to Malé for the supplies. One complete list with no room for error, every trip to Malé wasted two days of valuable time.

Mark, Wayne, Ryan, and Amy biked with them back to the boat. "What will we do while you are gone?" Mark asked a question that presented itself, desperate for suggestions.

Gamini spoke up before Bill could answer. "Go love them and learn from them. They will teach you much in two days." The men climbed aboard the boat and pushed off into the Indian Ocean.

The four of them stood with bikes in hand. "I thought we were here to teach them," Wayne was more confused than any of them of Gamini's response.

"We will go back and do as they do," Amy responded. "We will live as they live and bond with them. We aren't here to be over them, but to be a part of them." Amy was right. She knew what Gamini was asking of them.

"We don't speak their language how are we supposed to 'bond' without an interpreter?" Wayne was more focused on himself than the possibilities.

"Kindness has a language all its own." Amy wasn't going to waste time trying to explain anything else. She lifted herself up on the bike and peddled away.

The three men stood there with their mouths open. The brothers were still dumbfounded on what to do. Ryan, however, was simply in awe at Amy's determination and purpose. He wasn't sure what he was going to be doing, but he knew he wanted to be doing it beside Amy.

By the time the men caught up with Amy, she had parked her bike by their hut and had sought out someone to get to know. She had a gentle look and soft touch; she was so open to everyone. The easy place to go would be to Gamini's hut and hang out with his wife Ari, but not Amy. She stood by a small hut playing peek-a-boo with a child of maybe three or four. The girl's mother smiled as she watched the interaction with her daughter. Amy reached out to the mom and imitated the motions she was making. The mom moved over making room for Amy to sit down. They sat around a large basket filled with coarse fiber. The mom pulled, separated, and beat the material in the basket piece by piece. Amy wasn't sure what she was doing, but did her best to help. The mom took her hands and slowly moved them; they divided a handful into sections, twisted them and then laid them across a wooden table and began to beat the material with a stick, again and

39

again. The material was so rough, but the mom made it look so easy. When the coir fibers were beaten to a tender pliable consistency, six to ten stands were separated and the ends of these strands were joined to the ends of another few strands by spinning between the palms of their hands. A thick rope started to form as the fibers blended. Thirty minutes later, Amy's effort paid off with about ten inches of rope compared to the two feet of coir rope the mom had spun together. Amy flinched in pain as one of the fibers cut into the side of her hand and around into her palm. It was as if a knife was slicing her as she tightened the strands. With blood dripping off her palm, Amy pulled back and put pressure on the wound.

Ryan had been watching the whole time. He longed to be so open and able to reach out. He was quiet, slightly reserved, but willing. He could learn so much from Amy. He already knew that they would work well together if given a chance. In addition, if given a choice, he would choose to be on Amy's team. He saw Amy's hand bleeding and started toward her to help. The mom had been so focused on what she was doing that she hadn't realized Amy was hurt until she saw Ryan coming closer with a look of concern on his face. She took Amy by the hand and led her over to the side of the hut where there were barrels of fresh water. She took a clean cloth from the rack above the barrels and dipped it into the water. Amy let the woman take care of her. Her rough leather-like skin caressed the wound pulling loose fibers out as she wiped it clean. She motioned for Amy to stay and wait.

Ryan came around to Amy's side to look. "She is enjoying taking care of you." He saw the blisters rising on Amy's fingers. "You aren't use to manual labor are you?" Amy was looking down when Ryan commented. He bent down and raised her face to his. "I am teasing," Ryan said. He was shocked when he saw that her eyes were tear-filled. "I am sorry. I didn't mean to hurt your feelings." Ryan felt horrible and didn't know what to do. For some instinctive reason, he wanted to hug her as though it would take back his words and ease her pain.

"It's not you Ryan." Her hand was hurting. She didn't want to seem weak or useless. Nor did she want to disappoint the woman she was trying so hard to work with and get to know. "This is much harder than crocheting."

The mom came back holding what looked like half a coconut shell filled with a white pasty salve. She motioned for Amy's hand with firm aggression. "Ryan, is this safe?" Amy looked pitiful.

"I think you have to show her you trust her, Amy." Ryan didn't like not knowing what was in the salve. He kept thinking of how she had nursed Amy's hand already. He didn't feel a reason not to trust. "I am here for you; I will keep an eye on you." He hoped that it would bring some comfort.

"Aharenge namakee, Razan. Kon nameh Kiyanee," she said as she put the salve on the wound and the blisters. "Aharenge namakee, Razan" she said a second time, but this time she pointed to herself. "Kon nameh Kiyanee," she repeated looking at them.

"I believe she is trying to tell you her name, Amy. She is relating to you." Amy was focused on Razan as she finished applying the salve and wrapping a clean cloth around her hand and between her fingers. "Ryan," he said, pointing to himself. "Amy," he said motioning towards her. This action was repeated until they all seemed to have the correct enunciation.

Razan's daughter curiously approached them. "Meena," Razan called to her and then said something that neither of them understood. "Meena," she repeated. Amy and Ryan waved to Meena and called her by name. She ran away playfully. Razan put the shell of salve back in the hut. She came out focused and walked directly back to the basket of fiber.

"Looks like it's time to go back to work," Ryan said. "How does your hand feel?"

"Better, believe it or not. The salve smells like it has some sort of mint in it. It cooled and numbed my hand quickly."

Amy sat down beside Razan and assumed her previous position. Razan got frustrated immediately, motioning for Amy to leave and for Ryan to sit down. She pointed quickly between Meena and Amy. Just as quick, she pointed for Ryan to have a seat where Amy was made to get up. "Looks like it's your turn to twist, beat, and spin or whatever it is I was doing."

Amy got up and went to stand beside Meena. Ryan sat and watched Razan intently. He found a rhythm to what she was doing. He caught on so fast. When he looked up at Amy, she began acting jealous in a silly way. She may have been a little flirtatious too, although it's not something she would admit. Meena started mocking Amy's actions. They laughed at each other's expressions. Soon, it became a game of charades and giggling. They imitated birds, turtles, trees, and Ryan! He had no idea that he was biting his lip as he concentrated on the rope. Both girls bit their lip and pretended to be Ryan as he repeatedly beat the coir fibers. He looked up, caught their mimicking, and shook his head in embarrassment. Since they had been discovered, there was no longer a challenge so they found something else to occupy themselves. He watched Amy play with Meena. He saw Razan smile at his efforts to help. Gamini was very right; kindness has a universal language of its own.

The brothers came out of the hut one time looking for water. Ryan called out for them to come and learn a new occupation. They disappeared as quickly as they appeared. "They sure are peculiar," he thought to himself. He wouldn't see them again until dinner.

The smell of rice, sweet potatoes, and fresh fish filled the air. Islanders that they had not seen at all came from every direction when the large bell was rung. Some were shirtless, dirty, and smelly, all were hungry. The oldest males ate first. Respectfully, everyone waited their turn. Ryan and the brothers joined the men, but waited until Amy was served before they began to eat. Food never tasted better, they were so hungry. As teenagers, they missed the convenience of chips and candy bars whenever they wanted.

After dinner, all the young men who had apparently been working out on the fishing boats since dawn stayed around the small village. It was now Ryan's chance to reach out and to cross language barriers with kindness. Ryan felt really nervous when five men showed up with machetes. He didn't react to the men as they swung the machetes around seemingly hoping to get a rise out of the three new men. But, it made an impression on the brothers. As soon as there was an opening, they high-tailed it back to the hut. They were envisioning some sort of missionary sacrifice and didn't want to be any part of a tribal ritual. The village men laughed at the brother's reaction. They knew what they were doing. It was a game that the younger men like to play on anyone staying in their village. Ryan instantly had their respect as he sat there quietly, still and watching their every move.

Razan yelled at one young fellow who looked so much like her he had to be her son. He went into Razan's hut and returned with another machete. With machete in each hand, he stood in front of Ryan. He stood up looking the young man in the eye, not blinking; he waited for the young man's next move.

"Rafah," Razan was telling Ryan his name. Rafah gave a machete to Ryan and motioned for him to follow. This was getting more and more interesting. The brothers watched from the cutout window of their hut. They prayed that Ryan wasn't going to have to defend his life or become a sacrifice.

Ryan followed a group of young men about fifty yards to

a group of coconut palm trees. There were seven trees and seven men including Ryan. The six islanders slid their machetes between a rope and their pants. The machete was parallel with their back and legs. They stared at Ryan, waiting for him to do the same and he did.

As if they had done this a million times, the six men put one hand chest high and the other hand waist high on the other side of the tree. They jumped simultaneously, planting their feet on both sides of the tree with their knees perpendicular to their body. Their machetes dangled from behind them between their legs; they jumped up the tree like a frog. Ryan had never seen anything so funny looking before. They all reached the top in a matter of a minute and sat upon the fronds of the palm staring down at Ryan. He considered himself challenged by the men. This happened all the time back home in the States too. Who was stronger, faster, and braver, but the challenges didn't consist of climbing thirty feet with a sharp machete between your legs.

Amy was afraid for Ryan. She prayed for help out of this situation. Surely Ryan wouldn't be so full of testosterone that he would attempt this challenge. She was right; she didn't know Ryan that well because he was taking his belt loose and readjusting it to fit the machete behind him. Amy felt sick and sat down before she fainted. She wanted to yell at him but didn't want to embarrass him. He was focused like she had already seen him several times before. "Dear God help this craziness," she pleaded out loud. Only God understood her.

Ryan walked over to the palm and examined it in detail. The palm trees didn't have bark like the trees at home. There were sharp frond stubs all the way up the palm. "That's why they didn't hug the tree to climb up," Ryan thought. He touched the end of the frond and it poked him like a pin. The guys in the trees began to talk to each other. Ryan knew they were talking about him and betting whether or not he was going to attempt, much less succeed the climb.

He placed his hands on the palm just like he watched the others do. He tried to put one foot up and then the next but the fronds gave way causing his leg to slip. The frond caught his jeans and ripped the inseam. "Okay, this is why they jumped," he said aloud like he was instructing someone else. "Like a frog," with that he jumped and clung to the tree. His grip was good. He was strong in muscle and mind. "Speed is the key not to exhaust yourself," he mumbled. Jump, jump, jump and up, up, up he went.

Amy was amazed. The villagers watched and chanted with excitement as if they were all pulling for the crazy, brave American. When he reached the top, he pulled himself up and stood on the long fronds hoping that the others couldn't see his tired arms and legs shaking. He took the machete out of his belt and sat down. The other wasted no time in celebration. They took their machetes and starting whacking the longs fronds and letting them fall to the ground. Without thinking twice, Ryan did the same. He kept a slightly slower pace than the others which should be expected from someone who had never done this before, his ten to their fifteen, not too bad at all. Ryan watched as the men allowed their machetes to fall to the ground. He was very relieved that he didn't have to go down the palm with it in his belt. When all the machetes hit the ground, the teenage boys came to gather them and moved the freshly cut fronds away from the palm.

As Ryan looked down and watched the activity, he suddenly realized how high off the ground he was. He became a little queasy when he began to think about getting down. Suddenly the climb up seemed easier. The men lowered their bodies until their feet settled on the frond stubs. They positioned their hands the same as the climb up and began to jump down, froglike once again. Now it was Ryan's turn to pray. His braveness had disappeared in the clouds that hung

45

over his head. All eyes were on him. "Okay, here I go Lord. Be my strength." Ryan mimicked the maneuvers of the guys who went before him and in a flash, he was down the palm like he had the experience of all the others. Now the villagers were excited and celebrated him. The men who met him at the bottom of the palm patted his back like a puppy. That was their way of congratulating him. When the crowd dispersed, Amy ran to him, slugged him on the right arm, and then hugged him quickly, but with purpose.

"Ouch, what's that about," Ryan complained rubbing his arm as if Amy had actually hurt him.

"Don't you ever do that to me again!" Amy cried out. "I was so afraid for you. I about died of anxiety!"

"Well, I about died from being impaled by a palm tree! Take it easy on me," Ryan said, making light of Amy's worries. "We survived better than my pants did." He pointed to the tear from above his knee to mid-calf. "The first tear was half that size. I caught it again on the way down. I was so glad I was only five feet from the ground."

They started laughing. Partly because they didn't know how else to release their emotions and the other reason… they were starting to enjoy each other's company.

CHAPTER EIGHT

HARD WORK AND RESPECT

A good night's sleep was so needed. Still weary from travel, the day's events added to the need for rest. Ryan and Amy lay awake in separate areas. Their bodies were still, but their minds were in full motion. They thought about the day and the relationships they were forming with the islanders and each other. They were at peace with their decision to come to Maldives and comfortable with the work ahead of them. As sleep finally overcame them, dreams beyond Maldives filled their minds and hearts. A future, a goal and the possibility of unity that would last a life time, made it hard to wake up when the morning sun arose.

"Ryan, wake up man." Mark shook Ryan with more and more effort. "I think these men want you outside." Ryan did not want to open his eyes. He didn't want the visions that had made him feel so needed and loved to disappear. "I'm asking you to get up now, dude!" With that last plea, Mark yanked the sheets that Ryan was all wound up in, causing him to roll into the suitcases lined up against the wall.

"Ouch!" Ryan complained. "What's up?"

"You tell me. I got up to go to the restroom and there are

fifteen men standing in front of the hut. I don't think they are waiting to escort me to pee!"

Ryan knew Mark was truly concerned. "Calm down big boy. I'll see what's going on." He got up, slid his torn pants over his shorts, and grabbed for a shirt. "You just stay here. I'll take care of this." Mark nodded in full agreement. Ryan walked past the doorway of the young lady who was half responsible for his new energy and vision. He thought he would see her under a pile of covers sound asleep. To his surprise, the covers were folded and Amy was nowhere to be seen. His heart pounded for fear that something had happened to her while he slept.

The front of the hut was crowded with some of the same men that he had climbed the palm with the night before. They were glad to see him and tried in their own way to communicate their wishes, but Ryan was more focused on finding Amy. It was a tie concerning which of his senses took over the search. He tried to look over the men that he had apparently earned great respect from, but he couldn't see anything beyond their friendliness and desire to be with him. His sense of smell took over for his vision. The sweet aroma of fruit and a warm fire cooking something heightened. He turned toward the smoke and listened beyond his surroundings. He closed his eyes and tuned out every close sound. There she was. He couldn't see her, but he knew the sound of her voice already. She was helping Razan and the other women cook breakfast for the men getting ready to go out on the boats fishing.

Amy looked up to see Ryan's blue eyes reflecting relief. She took a plate and piled fruit, rice and nuts so high that she had to walk with great caution not to drop everything on her way over to him. "Good morning sleepy head." She smiled the same smile that he had often seen in his dreams from the night before.

"Do you normally wake up this early?" Ryan questioned as he took the plate. He offered a quick "thank you Lord for the food" and dug in unashamed of his hunger and lack of table manners. With the absence of a table and eating utensils, he figured his actions were acceptable.

"Slow down there Ryan, there are plenty of fruit-filled trees for you to climb. You aren't going to starve." Amy mocked his barbaric eating and laughed as the rice stuck to his razor stubble chin. "You are in high demand around here."

Amy knew something he didn't. She heard noises outside the hut thirty minutes before Ryan had appeared. When she went to check on everything, she saw the women gathering everything for breakfast. Razan was chatting with the others as Amy came closer. She could pick out Ryan's name on occasion. He was definitely the topic of conversation. Razan pulled Amy closer into the cooking area and unwrapped Amy's hand to take a look at the sores and cuts from yesterday. Two irritated lines were all that was left of the cuts and bruises she had less than twenty-four hours earlier. That satisfied Razan enough to motion for her to wash her hands and help with the cooking.

She did her best to look busy as she tried to piece together what was going on around her. Every other word seemed to be about Ryan. He had made quite an impression. As the men gathered for breakfast, their talk revolved around him too. Language may be a barrier, but expressions have a language of their own.

"Um, okay, just what does that mean?" Ryan asked, clearly puzzled.

"I think your day is planned out for you. Every time your name was mentioned, someone went to get more fishing nets or poles." Amy couldn't hold back a laugh as she told him that it looked like he was going tuna fishing today.

"I don't know a thing about fishing!" Ryan's voice

cracked as he accidently spewed rice from his mouth.

"Are you going to tell them no? They think you are a super hero." Amy was being sarcastic, but Ryan was serious.

"I wasn't the most comfortable on the ride here," Ryan admitted. "Have you seen those boats they use for fishing?" Ryan took a deep breath that was followed by a heavy sigh. He swallowed the rest of his breakfast without tasting it. "Okay, everything will be fine. I will give it my best."

Somewhere between his lack of fishing experience, being out on the ocean all day and that deep breath, he had found peace. "How do you do that Ryan?" Amy had softened her voice. She wanted a serious answer.

Ryan didn't tease her or make light of her question. He knew what she was asking. "Amy, I am nothing within myself. A couple of years ago, I was introduced to a love that I never knew before. It was the unconditional love of God. People who didn't know me or owe me anything made me believe that I was worth loving by their actions. They didn't let any barriers stand between us. I want that same unconditional love to show through me to these people. I will use my strength to love and honor them."

Ryan could see Amy had more to say. He waited patiently for her to form her thoughts into words. All she finally voiced sounded so frail and concerned. "Aren't you afraid?"

"Silly lady, there is no fear in love." Ryan handed the plate back to her as the men gathered their nets and equipment to head out to the docks. "Stay close to Razan. She will keep you busy and take care of you," he instructed. He smiled a different kind of smile to her, or at least she thought he did. His smile seemed warm and caring, quiet and gentle, as if a smile could show emotion of its very own, or speak a thousand words to her. She prayed that she was actually seeing his feelings and not her own desires.

Ryan saw the pile of thick coir ropes. He threw two ropes

over each shoulder and picked up a box of tools lying beside them. He was clueless on what any of these things were for, but he was willing to find out. Razan called his name as best she could. He turned to find her trying to chase him down. She brought him a bag of food and a large jug of water. He was carrying more than his own weight in equipment and food, but that did not slow him down.

He also did not turn to look towards Amy again. It's not that he was ignoring her, but he never imagined that she would still be watching him. "You are more special than you know, Ryan." Amy's words were heard only by ears that didn't understand.

Amy's day consisted of following Razan to the marshes to gather reeds and vegetables for dinner. As they entered one particular portion of the marsh, she saw sticks poking up all around. The tip ends were apparently color-coated. Razan, Ari and several other women walked over to the sticks that were color- coated green and started digging with small trowels. Razan pointed to Amy and motioned toward the empty baskets. Amy carried one at a time over to the women. The work seemed back breaking as they bent from the waist to dig, holding up any of their loose clothing so they would not get covered in the mud. Slowly, round, nasty, mud-covered blobs were dug up and placed in the basket. When one was full, Amy went to get another. The sticks were pulled up and stacked on dry ground. The rounded masses were unidentifiable. Three baskets seemed enough for the day. They took the baskets over to the water edge and started rinsing away the mud. To Amy's surprise, the round objects were coconut shells. The fibers had loosened from around the shell and were sticking up everywhere. It made the coconuts look like they were having a very bad hair day.

They stacked reeds, gathered the fresh vegetables and fruits, and carried the baskets of coconuts back to the village.

51

After putting their day's collections away, they divided into two groups. One group of women made more coir rope and the other used the dry reeds for mat weaving. She liked the mat weaving much better than making rope. It wasn't as hard or as harsh on her hands. Amy wasn't aware that the women didn't trust her soft hands to make rope and that was the true reason they showed her how to weave. She wasn't offended at all. When the group she was with disbanded to make lunch, Amy took the time to play with Meena. The longer the two of them played, the more children that seemed to appear out of nowhere. It was exhausting and energizing at the same time. Amy had become their new toy.

After lunch, Amy brought out her yarn and crocheting hooks. The curious children gathered first, followed by some of their moms. Because the women already knew how to make rope and weave mats, crocheting techniques came easy for them. Amy had them all excited about the bright colors of yarn she had brought with her. The easiest things to make would be bracelets. Before long, every little girl and woman had made at least one double chain bracelet and were wearing them with pride. Amy's only regret is that she hadn't brought more yarn with her.

Ryan had never worked harder in his life. Pole fishing for tuna and fighting with each individual tuna that grabbed hold of his hook was challenging. Laying out the large heavy nets, balancing the small boats in the sometimes turbulent Indian Ocean currents, pulling the heavy catches up and separating out which fish to keep and which to throw back. Every muscle in his body ached, but he found he loved every minute of it!

After returning and docking the boats, Ryan saw a ferry in the distance. He had hoped it was Bill and Gamini returning with supplies. He decided to wait instead of going back to the village with the others. "Hey Bill, how was your trip?" Ryan yelled out. He was excited to see Bill again. He walked out to grab the guide wire of the ferry and help to pull it closer to the dock.

"Interesting, Ryan, it's always interesting when you go into the mainland." Bill left it at that, but Ryan could tell from his tone that there was so much more to what he was saying.

"Nice ride," Ryan teased pointing to the ferry.

"Thanks, we needed something big enough to hold all the supplies. Grab a load and let's go. I'm hungry." Bill filled his arms up and led the way with Gamini and Ryan close behind. They loaded the carts and attached them to the bikes parked close by.

Amy waited impatiently at the edge of the village for Ryan. She was nervous not knowing why he didn't come back with the others. Seeing him riding the bikes back with Bill and Gamini made her realize her being led to the islands of Maldives had many purposes. She was reaching out, loving the people, helping whenever possible, but God was also blessing her as she blessed others. 'That is how God works' was the phrase Ryan used often when trying to explain God's unseen plan working in people's lives. Sometimes there wasn't an explanation that seemed suitable for God's grace, so Ryan's phrase started making sense.

Dinner was about done. Even if Amy could have hugged Ryan, she would have to refrain. The man truly stunk. Between the hot sun, fishing and hard work, Ryan smelled as bad as dinner smelled great. Amy insisted Ryan shower before they ate and she promised not to talk about anything with Bill until later.

The brothers made an appearance at dinner time. They greeted Bill and Gamini. They were suddenly talkative.

After dinner, the same six that doubted Ryan's strength and bravery yesterday, came back with the machetes for another climb. This time, he was an equal.

Another set of palm trees was grouped at the south side of the village. There were more trees than climbers this time. They all chose trees closest to each other. With machetes in place and eye contact made, a head nod of the oldest climber sent them all leapfrogging up the tree. Ryan stayed right with them the whole way up. The transition to the top of the fronds was smooth. Within two minutes of leaving the ground, they were all whacking palm branches off and throwing them to the ground. This time, they added collecting coconuts to the climb. Something else Ryan had to learn to do. He watched as the men bent over the top of the palm and reached down to the coconuts as they wrapped their legs around the palm branches to hold on. They twisted once, twice, and with a quick snap and pull, the coconut was in their hands. Fifteen branches to thirteen branches were too good for the guys so they had to offer another challenge. Ryan thought for a minute and strategically cut away two more branches. He spread his feet as wide as he could and still have good balance. He raised the machete above his head and with two fast whacks, four coconuts fell to the ground. He was not going to bend over the tree and dangle for coconuts. As the others finished pulling the coconuts off the palm, Ryan threw his machete down first then leapfrogged down the tree. Soon after, the other machetes were tossed down and the guys followed. The seven of them were all energy-filled bundles of strength. Testosterone must have a universal language of its own also.

Bill laughed the whole time. He was pleased at the way Ryan and Amy had interacted with the villagers. Although the brothers were different, Bill knew they were there for a purpose too. They would show their talents later.

Chapter Nine

Love and Works

The cool of the evening had quietly arrived on the island and the village started to settle down. The five Americans joined Gamini in his hut. His wife, young son, and teenage daughter joined them in the common room. The brothers had brought their instruments. That was the first time they had them out since customs had pulled all their belongings out on the tables. Gamini's hut was nice. It had thick mud walls that had been perfectly smoothed out when it was built. There were actual walls that divided the rooms. The common room and kitchen both had small cut-out windows. They closed the thin window covering for some privacy.

Gamini spoke softly at first. "You will play music with my children. Explore their songs, teach instruments and whatever need is to keep a busy noise. Do you have paper?"

This was the time that they all had been waiting on. The brothers knew they had something important on them, but didn't know what or where. Ryan and Amy knew there was a mission involved somewhere too. The mystery was about to be solved.

"Wayne, hand me your bongos." Bill took the bongos from Wayne and turned them upside down. He put his hand inside the opening and felt around. "No, not there," he said. "Hand me the other one." Wayne did as he asked. Bill did the same thing, but this time he began gently pulling something from inside the bongo, first one side and then the other. Taped to each wall was an envelope. He handed the bongos back to Wayne. When he opened the envelopes, Gamini gasped.

"This is it? This is the words you speak of to me?" He was so excited and childlike. He asked Bill if he could hold the papers. Tears came to his eyes as he held the papers to his chest. "Thank you God! Thank you God!" Gamini took the papers away from his chest and kissed them. His hands shook as if he were holding precious gems. He kissed the papers again. Expressive sounds of praise rose up from his very soul. The Americans didn't need to understand his words. They understood his heart. They watched him as he was unashamed of his tears and worship. Amy cried with him. If they would leave at this moment, they already knew a life had been changed for eternity by their efforts.

Ryan tried to see what Gamini had, but could not. He mouthed the words "What is it" to Bill. He got up and moved closer to the others. "It's the first thirteen chapters of Luke. Gamini has never seen a Bible before." They all watched Gamini as he held the pages so carefully as if they were his most valuable possession. "There are not any Bibles translated into the Dhivehi language, which is why we are here."

Softly, Wayne started tapping on the bongo. Mark picked out a harmonica and reverently started playing to the tune of Amazing Grace. Daring not to sing the words, the others hummed the tune with them in worship. None of them had ever seen such a response to a person seeing God's word before. It didn't matter that it was only half of a book either.

The pages were holy in the hands of Gamini. Fifteen minutes passed, Gamini continued his silent praise and thankfulness to God as the tears that were dammed up in his eyes, finally spilled over. The rest of the world didn't exist right now. They were all in the presence of God as Gamini whispered prayers and the others hummed in worship.

Ira could no longer hold their curious kids back. Mifrah, their four year old son, burst into the room running straight for his father. Gamini opened his eyes to see his boy staring, not understanding the emotion he was witnessing from his father. Sana, their thirteen year old daughter, watched the faces of those worshipping. She was nervous and uncertain of what was happening at first, but the peace in that room was undeniable. She didn't want to leave. Amy motioned for her to sit down beside her. Gamini hugged his son and reached out for his wife. Ira came to him sensing the same presence of a God. This night would be remembered by everyone in that room eternally.

That is how the next two weeks went. Every day they were up early and straight to work on the new building. The Americans were joined by the village men who Ryan had befriended during his tree climbing and fishing ventures. Respect bonded them.

Ryan's group was in charge of cutting down what the islanders called Jamdul or Dhanvah, which were simply trees. This wood was to be used for framing and boat-building, because it was durable and it was water and termite resistant. Of course, there were palm branches that needed to be cut for the roof. This became a game to the men. The competition always came down to two men, Ryan and Arzan. When the two of them climbed, all the others watched to see who would stand first at the top of the palm tree. The two young men were definitely well-matched in strength and ability. The brothers, Gamini and Bill did the framing and building of the walls.

Amy went with the women every morning to gather reeds for the mat weaving and extra for the building. Other village women continued making the coir rope. Amy was invited to go back to the marshes this time carrying baskets of freshly hulled-out coconut. She didn't understand this process at all. Each of the women grabbed a yellow-tipped stick and began burying the shells and marking the place with the stick. She later asked Gamini the purpose of the whole bury and dig up procedures. He explained that burying the coconut shells in the mud for a couple of months was a way to loosen the coir fibers from the shell. It all began to make sense then. Amy finally understood how the fibers were pulled from the shell and softened by beating them, but they never did give Amy another chance at rope making. Mat weaving was all they trusted her to do during the rest of her visit.

CHAPTER TEN

RELATIONSHIPS OF MANY

No one worked after dinner. Gamini would take Ryan, Amy, and Bill to explore the island. Sometimes Gamini's family or some village children would join them. The children were particularly drawn to Amy. She was very attentive and loving toward them. The brothers, who were less adapted to all the physical work, chose to use this time to rest.

Fuvahmulah was so beautiful and unique. It was the second-largest island in Maldives at only 2.8 miles long and 0.7 miles wide. There was so much to appreciate about the island. It was so diverse with tropical wetlands, freshwater lakes, well-vegetated marshlands and a variety of beaches. It was the beaches that marveled Amy. She walked beside Ryan every night, regardless of who else tagged along. The north part of the island had white sandy beaches. In the southwest corner of Fuvahmulah was the village of Dandigan. On their beaches Amy found kalho-akiri which meant black pebbles. Each visit, Amy would pick up a pebble and keep it as a memory.

The month of August was still in the thick of the southwest monsoon season. The weather was either perfectly beautiful or perfectly stormy. Storms could pop up quickly.

Whenever they set up for the day's work, they had to be wise and plan for, at the minimum, a shower to slow down progress. Sometimes they faced a full-blown tropical storm that might shut them down for a couple of days. So far they had been blessed by having only one storm to shut them down longer than a day. That stormy day was Ryan's favorite memory.

After dinner, the usual group took a walk, but this time the brothers joined them. They had only walked about a half mile before the winds started picking up. In a matter of minutes, the rains came pelting down on them so hard that it hurt to the point of stinging. Ryan was sure that the brothers had never moved so fast in their lives. Their long, lanky legs tried to escape, but the sand became a vacuum to their footing causing them to both sink and slip with every step they took. Bill chose to walk briskly back to the village, leaving Ryan and Amy to seemingly fend for themselves. Bill knew Ryan would take care of Amy. He had noticed the attraction between the two of them, and a little time together would be okay. The storm didn't seem to be one that was going to last long.

By the beach, there was no place to go for protection. Amy never complained, but Ryan knew she was hurting. He guided her to a line of trees and motioned for her to stay there. Twenty yards away, a small fishing boat was tied to a post. Ryan ran and emptied the boat of the water that had already filled the bottom. He bent his legs and reached for the crossbars. On his first try, Ryan failed to get the boat to release from the sand's grip. The rain was as relentless as Ryan's efforts. Again, to no avail, he lifted the boat by its crossbars only to fall into the boat this time. More determined than ever, he got out of the boat and pulled it inland until the suction let loose. He picked the boat completely up and over his head and carried it to the tree line where Amy waited. He broke off two long tree branches, shoved them into the sand, and propped up the boat for shelter. Amy and Ryan crawled under the boat, relived and out of the rain. Their skin tingled from the stinging rain. The metal-bottomed boat offered shelter; however the hard rain vibrated and pounded on it so hard that it was almost deafening. They were 'forced' to sit close to each other if they were going to be able to have any kind of conversation.

"How are you holding up?" Ryan had to repeat twice, and then decided to scoot even closer.

"I am good. Thank you for the protection. You looked caveman-ish out there man-handling the boat." Ryan thought about what Amy just said as they tried to wipe some of the wetness from their face and arms.

"I didn't pound my chest and grunt, but I felt very successful being able to pick this thing up and carry it over here." Ryan actually blushed when he talked to Amy. "Me have woman to protect!" With that he did beat his chest and grunt. They both had a good laugh.

The storm lasted one hour and thirty-four minutes to the second. Ryan and Amy had such a good talk under that small boat. After the storm clouds rolled away, the sun shined as brightly as if it had never rained. Amy insisted on helping him carry the boat back to the beach and tie it up. The others came looking for them as they tied the last knot.

"What did you two do, go out for a little row while it stormed?" Mark always had to be the wise-guy.

"Sure did, Mark," Amy quipped back. "We weren't wet enough where we were." She always seemed to be the one to put Mark in his place. Mark took it in stride and awaited another opportunity to insert his sarcasm again.

Their last week was approaching fast. Eight days left and so much left to do. The building was coming along great. There was no doubt that it would be done. The problem was in translating the Bible. The writing and language was so different. Every word took time to transpose. The late hours at Gamini's were difficult after working all day on the building.

Their bodies were so tired. They prayed nightly for God to strengthen their bodies and minds. This one night in particular became the brother's favorite memory.

They had gathered in Gamini's hut like they had every night. This night the hut was filled with exhausted people. Their bodies and minds were weary, but here was so much to do that they came faithfully to stay on course. The brothers had been playing and teaching Mifrah and Sana the bongos and harmonica as part of their nightly meetings. For the most part, it was 'making a joyful noise unto the Lord' because calling it music would be stretching it way too far. Wayne picked up both sets of bongos and handed one directly to Mifrah. Mark let Sana choose whichever harmonica she wanted and sat down against the walls. Tap, tap, Wayne started and Mifrah mocked his every beat. Sana picked out her favorite harmonica, put it to her mouth, and folded her right hand over the harmonica forming a tight cup. With a deep inhale, Sana blew longingly into the instrument waving her hand against the back. The reeds started vibrating, creating a soft sound. Then she inhaled through the harmonica, this time continuing to wave her hand across the back. The noise had become music. Mark joined Sana on his harmonica and Amazing Grace sounded... amazing.

However, the soft praise only lasted about ten minutes before Mifrah decided he had enough of the soft sounds. The four year old started tapping faster and faster. He wanted to free style tonight. He got happy feet as he had every limb and appendage moving with a beat. He was so funny. They all watched as the little one's facial expressions changed from sweet to radical as the beat got faster. Mark and Wayne were able to keep up and still manage to make music out of the boys' beats. Sana had to give up. She was laughing so hard at her brother that she couldn't breathe to play anymore. There wasn't any translating the Bible on this night. It was free styled laughter and joy. It was good for them to laugh because they had been carrying such a big burden. When their sides hurt from laughing so hard, they called it a night. Sleep was easy that night.

CHAPTER ELEVEN

WHEN EVIL VISITS

The sunset was spectacular, as usual. The ocean seemed still as the waves breached the shores peacefully. The turquoise colors in the water reflected the orange and red tones of the sun. The waves crept toward their feet reaching out for their toes. There they stood, all five American's with Gamini and his family, their shadows cast them as tall as giants and lay in perfect form on the sand. They were all deep in thought of God as they were in awe of His creation. Not once during their stay had they taken this view for granted.

Three days and two nights were all there was left. With one of the days being needed for travel back to Malé, their time was even shorter. The building was finished and beautiful. The new community facility was by far the sturdiest and most modern place on the island. The main entrance led into the common room that was twenty five by twenty five foot. Another smaller room was on the south side of the building; it was twenty five by fifteen foot, with a hallway that led to a closet area and an entire wall of shelves. On the north side of the common room was a hallway that divided seven rooms on each side of the hall. Fourteen ten by twelve foot rooms were big enough to be used as bedrooms, hospital rooms, or small classrooms. A multipurpose building was what they wanted and what they got.

The tiny voice of Meena broke the silence they were all sharing. The little girl that Amy had first played with was running toward them with a panicked look as she called out for her. Amy walked toward her and Meena jumped up into her arms, talking so fast that even if Amy could have understood the language, she wouldn't have been able to understand what Meena was saying. Gamini listened to her and interpreted for her.

"The National Security Service is at the village. They are asking questions about you all. We must go back." Gamini led the Americans. He gave them the best advice he could. "Do no give any information. Speak only when they ask." His advice was short and straight to the point. They walked with urgency, trying not to show the fear they felt.

There were four of them and they were armed, which wasn't unusual. The National Security Service acted as the police, military, and coast guard. With Britain no longer offering military stability, the N.S.S was in charge of it all. They felt the easiest way to deal with crime was to act fast and harsh. No judge, no jury; the National Security Service was the enforcer and interpreter of the law. Gamini met the men and spoke in Dhivehi. The conversation wasn't without conflict. The security service men kept pointing at Gamini and then the Americans. Gamini smiled nervously at them and pointed to the community building that they had just finished. Back and forth with their questions and then Gamini's answers. Two guards separated themselves. One guard went into Gamini's hut and one into the American's hut. They pulled out books, emptied shelves and tore off all the bed clothes off the pallets. They tore through more in fifteen minutes than could be repaired in hours. Someone had been talking about the

Americans and Gamini to the officials. They were speculating about why they spent so much time together. Islamic laws were not being upheld and someone had to pay the price.

Amy held tightly to Meena. She felt the fear radiate out from her little body. Standing behind all the men and watching the confrontation was too much for Amy as well. She hugged Meena to herself and put her head over her shoulder. She ran her fingers calmly through the darkness of Meena's hair and whispered a prayer in her ears for all of their safety. Meena did not understand a word, but she felt safe in Amy's arms. She never turned around again. She wanted Amy to hold her; she trusted Amy.

The two guards questioning Gamini got closer and closer to him. Bill couldn't tell if they were accusing him or just intimidating him. It was actually both. One guard got right up in Gamini's face while the other walked around looking at the Americans. He was so close to them that they could feel his breath on them. The guard with Gamini became very agitated with him and took a step back putting his hand on his handgun. His voice got louder and louder. Ryan didn't like what he was seeing and took a step toward the guard.

Arzan appeared out of nowhere and pulled Ryan back forcefully. He walked toward the guard pointing and laughing at the American's. He started talking, trying to change the mood of the guards. The guards knew Arzan. His grandfather was part of the village council. The guards finally settled down and started bantering with him. Whatever Arzan said made sense to the guards. Their tense angry faces eased up.

"Enough waste of time," the older guard called to the others. "Any finds?" He questioned the other guards who had not found anything illegal. The guards decided to leave. The guard had two more questions for Gamini before he left. One being, "When are the Americans leaving?" and two, "Did he want to die?"

"Saturday" and "No" were again the short and to-the-point answers from Gamini. He stood his ground proudly, or foolishly, as some might say.

The guards left, but not before stopping in front of Bill and the other Americans, "Make sure you leave." His voice rang out with a threatening tone. They didn't need an interpreter, no one answered him. They left without another word.

As soon as the guards were out of sight, Gamini and Bill both ran into their huts to survey the damage and look for all the work they had done while translating the Bible. Bill came back to the doorway and dropped to his knees. Both bongos were missing. All their work was gone.

Meena then climbed down out of Amy's arms and took her by the hand. She led Amy into her hut and called out for her mother. Razan slid out from behind a stack of mats that she had made to be taken to market. She walked to the door and looked around. She saw Gamini and ran to him. They spoke briefly and soon walked toward Razan's hut where Amy was with Meena. Gamini motioned for Bill to join them.

As Razan spoke, Gamini translated. "The guards came looking for Americans who build and play music. Razan say someone came to tell council of mystery. Why they here? Why Americans give so much? They suspect things." Razan went to the mats and slid them back from the wall. Both bongos were there hidden.

Gamini continued translating. "We love your music. Meena listen and go to sleep humming you play at night. We fear they take away music we love so Meena go in and get these out to be safety."

He asked Razan some questions and seemed uneasy about her answers. Gamini told Bill that from what she understood, someone went to security about them. "We will have to stop now. Security will be back more and time no one know. Once they have question, they will return to see more. Things more danger now. More danger because they already question me and family faith to Islam." Gamini shook his head. He was more than a little concerned for everyone's safety.

"It's ok Gamini," Bill put his hand on his shoulder. Bill was the one responsible and he had to remember that Gamini's faith was new. "We are done this trip. You ok?"

Gamini looked relieved. He believed his friend's words. "No more this trip," meant to him that they weren't giving up, but were good to stop now.

"What do we do now Bill? We have time left here on the island." Wayne felt uneasy. Flashbacks of trouble going through customs at the airport started pounding in his head. "We can't just stand around here. Can we take the ferry back to Malé in the morning?"

"No, Wayne. We can't pack up and go. We would not have any place to stay in Malé anyway. Besides that, we have worked too hard to build relationships here just to leave. We aren't going to just stand around here. We were called here for three very distinct reasons; first, to love these people unconditionally, second, to build a building, and third, to translate the Bible. We have done our best. We may not be able to do more Bible translating, but we can continue to love them. And love them they did.

CHAPTER TWELVE

BETRAYED AND FORGIVEN

Wayne and Mark brought their instruments out that night. Through Gamini, they invited those interested to come and play music with them. "You will have many come to play," warned Gamini. "We love Bodu Beru on the islands." The brothers didn't know what that meant, but they would soon find out.

Soon, men carrying three large drums gathered. Another group of men with bells and others with these small sticks of bamboo with horizontal grooves followed. "Wow!" Mark and Wayne said simultaneously. "Where did all these people come from?"

Gamini laughed. "I warned you my friends. Bodu Beru is dance music. These men come to play and dance. They hear you many nights with your music. Now, since you invite them, they come to share with you."

"Why do they have those bamboo sticks?" asked Mark.

"They are called onugandu," answered Gamini. "It make sound of islands for dance. Let them play and if you want, join them."

About fifteen men had lined up around the brothers.

They started first with a real slow beat and tingling bells. The beat got faster and faster. Soon everyone who heard the music had feet that were tapping to the beat. Wayne joined in with his bongos. As the music got louder and faster, Mark joined in with the harmonica. The men danced tirelessly. It was like a big party as the crowds gathered to watch. It seemed as though the whole village was outside watching the performance. It was crazy, lively and nothing like the Americans had ever witnessed before. They were all having so much fun. After two hours, they were all so exhausted that it was time to say goodnight.

Gamini spoke with the musicians and the dancers as the others went to bed. They all felt a sense of accomplishment. The building was done. The people of the island knew they were loved and served by the Americans. Bill was right. They hadn't gotten as far on translating the Bible as they had hoped, but that part was in God's hands. He would have to make a way through what seemed like impossible odds and they all knew He would.

Rain, rain and more rain, the whole day was awash with a tropical storm. The Americans used this day to rest, pray, and pack. Bill sat in the common room looking through the papers that Gamini and he had worked so hard on. He paused when he realized how God was leaving a sweet message with all of them through His word. It was a confirmation of sorts to their whole mission there. He called for the others to join him. He had just began to share his inspiration with them when Gamini came knocking. He was checking to see if the Americans had enough to eat while the storm raged outside.

"Gamini, join us. I need to share what the Lord showed me today. The six of them gathered in the common room and sat on the ground, curious to hear what Bill had discovered. "Gamini, do you remember what scriptures we were working on last time we were together?"

"No, Bill I am sorry. I do not. It seems hard to translate so I think more on words to translate, not what words are meaning." Gamini seemed hesitant to admit this to them.

"God has sent us a reminder. I know we didn't get as far as we wanted in translating, but it is where we left off that has spoken to me." Bill adjusted the pages. "I know we came here with the hopes of getting through half of St. Luke's gospel, but I must tell you, we have not failed. We have translated through Luke chapter nine and verse seventeen which is the story of Jesus feeding the five thousand plus with only five loaves and two fishes." Bill waited to hear or see a response from those listening.

"We all know that story, Bill. It is a great miracle of Jesus, however we brought thirteen chapters. We barely made it into chapter nine." Mark was discouraged. He wanted it all done.

"Exactly, you see," Bill said with conviction looking them each in the eye, "It's not what we didn't accomplish, but what we did accomplish that will feed the people of Maldives spiritually. Whatever we have will be enough for God to use until He opens another door." Bill was thrilled with what the Lord had revealed to him. He too had been feeling like a failure until God revealed that he uses what we have to perform miracles. They had to trust and believe. Bill had just put the papers away in the men's bedroom when another knock came to the door. It was Arzan.

Gamini and Arzan spoke for a minute. "Arzan has something for me to tell you." Arzan had been a fierce competitor against Ryan. He challenged him at everything from climbing the palms, swinging machetes to balancing on the edge of a fishing boat in the Indian Ocean. Ryan never questioned Arzan's challenges. He didn't accept the challenges to beat him. He accepted the challenges to form a relationship with him and earn his respect.

Arzan started talking and Gamini translated. "I bring

sorry words to your group. I bring sorry words to you, Ryan."

When Ryan heard his name, he looked at them puzzled. "I don't know why you would owe me any apologies," Ryan said.

Gamini repeated Ryan's words to Arzan. The incredibly strong and proud young man hung his head and told Gamini why he was ashamed of himself. Gamini listened and seemed angry at first. When he had heard the whole story in Dhivehi and then in English, he simply told Arzan he was… "Forgiven." Gamini told Arzan that he could leave and he would tell his story to the Americans, but he wanted to stay. Whatever he had done, he wanted them to see he was sorry.

"Arzan was the one who went to his grandfather and complained about you Americans." Gamini explained. "He didn't trust your reasons for being here." They all turned and looked toward Arzan. He expected retaliation, but instead, received "Oks" from the brothers and Bill. Arzan was relieved that they didn't seem to hate him. However, there was more. He wanted Ryan to know everything.

He went on explaining things to Gamini. He confessed deeper his mistrust of the Americans, especially Ryan. "Arzan wants to know why you, Ryan, want to be here," translated Gamini. "He says you are smart and much talent to be here with us village when you don't know us. He doesn't understand your acceptance."

Then Gamini explained Arzan's jealousy and mistrust of Ryan. All eyes turned to Ryan. Arzan wanted a response.

Ryan did not hesitate. He knew the reason he was here. From the first time Gamini had told them to love the villagers, he took that as his personal mission. "I don't have to know you to care about you."

Arzan looked at Ryan. He knew there was more to what was going on. The spirit of God filled the little hut as Arzan stood there speechless. Finally, not knowing what to do or how to feel, he left the hut.

Little did they know that several weeks later, Arzan would be Gamini's first convert outside of his own family. Within two years, Arzan would also be the first martyr. He would be taken out into the Indian Ocean and told to deny this 'false' God, which he refused. He would be accused of luring Muslims from Islam to Christianity. A large stone would be tied to his feet and then he would be thrown over the side of the boat. Only Gamini would know the truth of what happened to Arzan. The National Security Service would not admit that even one Christian abided in Maldives, so there would be no report of his death, only his disappearance. Taking the life of Arzan would also be an informal warning to Gamini.

The rain poured all night and into the next day. Finally, the sun appeared. It was their last day on Fuvahmulah Island. The villagers knew it too. All day little gifts were brought to them. Each brother was brought the onugandu instrument from the musicians they played with two nights ago. Razan brought Amy a mat that she had weaved for her. The colors were perfect and every stitch tightly woven. The mat was so well made that it would last a lifetime. Bill was brought five feet of coir rope, like he had used to tie the corners of the building together.

Ryan, standing in the background and always watching, was flooded with love and appreciation for this village and its people. He hated the thought of leaving. He was spotted by Meena who called his name aloud and pointed her little finger in his direction. All six men he climbed and fished with, came walking toward him. In three lines, there were three men, then two men and in the back, Arzan. As they got to Ryan, they stepped aside to let Arzan stand directly in front of Ryan. Proudly, he held out a machete as a gift to Ryan. It was not just any machete either. Arzan handed him his own machete.

Ryan was receiving a very high honor. He accepted, nodded his head, and said but one word…"Brother."

Gamini would later translate that word for Arzan.

The last night was spent in music and celebration.

Bill awoke in a sweat. He had a dream about the Bible pages being found in the bongos. They had to come up with another hiding place quickly. The others started stirring as Bill paced the room praying about where to hide the priceless pages. Amy's voice rang out from the other room.

"Are you sleepy heads awake?" She asked knowing their time was short to get to the dock.

"UGH!" Wayne started complaining once again about Amy's early morning ritual. "Doesn't she believe in sleep?"

"If you sleep much longer, the boat will leave without you. You may be a good swimmer, but I don't think you will make it to Malé before the plane leaves tomorrow afternoon. So, get up!" With that, Mark threw his pillow at Wayne, smacking him square in the head.

Now that they were all awake, they noticed Bill's worried face. After questioning with "why the worried face", Bill explained his dream. "Where is a safe place?" They all thought long and hard as they packed.

CHAPTER THIRTEEN

BROTHER

The goodbyes were quick as time got away from them while they struggled with where to put the pages of the Bible. Most of the villagers walked with them to the dock. One important figure was missing, Arzan. As the others walked on, Ryan pleaded his case with Bill to let him find Arzan. "The boat will not wait on you," was Bill's firm warning. Ryan gave his things to the brothers and took off running toward Arzan's hut. He found him standing at the door, alone. Ryan had sought him out. He had stayed with him and accepted every task that Arzan had challenged him with. He had to say goodbye. He walked to Arzan, not sure what to do now. He realized that he should have thought about that before he got to him.

They both stood straight looking at each other with respect and honor. Five seconds, ten seconds, neither moved nor spoke a word. Finally, in as plain English as any American, Arzan said, "Brother."

Ryan repeated the endearment to him and turned to run to the dock.

The boat was pushing off the dock as Ryan ran out to the

beach. Still twenty five yards to go, but Ryan had no intention of swimming to Malé. The villagers saw him and began to shout. The Americans saw him too, but the rule was, the boat waits on no one.

Ryan's adrenaline increased one hundred percent. His strides burst into pure energy excelled. He was running so fast that the sand didn't have time to react to his footsteps. Onto the dock he jumped. The boat had edged a good fifteen feet away. "Make way," Ryan yelled as he took his last steps on solid ground before thrusting himself into the air and landing on the boat still running. Mark and Wayne had to body block him to keep him from running off the far side of the boat.

All the Americans stood at the stern of the boat. They waved goodbye as long as their arms would let them and when their arms finally gave out, they stood there until the island could no longer be seen. The men all left Amy standing to herself as she couldn't bear to look away. So many thoughts ran rampantly in her mind. She prayed and called everyone she had met by name. She wanted to make sure that God knew exactly who she was talking about, temporarily forgetting that He is their Heavenly Father and He knew them first, and loved them even more.

"How are you holding up, Amy?" Bill came to comfort her.

"I miss them already. How can that be?" Amy never turned to look at Bill for fear she would lose what little composure she had left in her.

Bill understood what she was saying. "You have loved them with the love of God. That is a deeper love than any of them have ever known. You gave completely of yourself. You will always miss them."

"Yes, Bill, I will always miss them. May I ask you a question?" The need for knowledge came alive. There were so many questions that she dared not ask on the island. So much she wanted to know.

"Sure," Bill said. "Anything"

"Why was St. Luke chosen?" Now Amy turned away from the direction of the island, and was ready for conversation.

"I was wondering the same thing." It was Ryan. He saw Bill talking to Amy, figured Amy had come to grips with her emotions, so they could all talk now.

"A lot of prayer went into the decision to translate St. Luke. The four gospels cover the events of Jesus' life and death. However, the disciples all had different backgrounds so they paid more attention to details that they related to. Luke was a physician. His family was educated and cultured. He knew well of the hatred of the Jews for the Gentiles. He often pointed this out because he was a Gentile and Jesus was a Jew. Jesus should have never spoken to the Gentiles, yet he traveled, ate, slept, and performed miracles on them. Luke was mindful of how Jesus treated the so-called second-class people. They moved to the bench on the side of the boat. Bill proceeded to explain that translating the Book of Acts is also part of the plan.

"Luke wrote Acts too. This also made him a better choice. In Acts, he writes about how the Holy Spirit is here to minister to everyone. The Spirit shows no partially, just like Jesus." Bill shared more details throughout the trip to Malé. As the darkness overtook the sky, they all settled down for the night. Ryan purposefully positioned himself by Bill. As the others fell to sleep, Ryan whispered to Bill.

"You awake?" It was the kind of whisper that, if Bill was already asleep, was meant to wake him up.

"I thought I was." Bill rolled over onto his back. "You want something?"

"I have a question. Now that you have the translation of some of Luke, what are you going to do with it? Ryan was curious of the next steps.

"I have to find someone to print the books, which will be the easy part. The hard part is getting the Bibles back into Maldives. I do not know how God is going to work that out. I am taking one blind step of faith at a time." Bill paused before admitting to Ryan that those concerns were in the future, his biggest concern was about tomorrow afternoon at the Malé airport.

"Why is that Bill? I thought you had found a place for the Bible pages." Ryan was confused.

"Ryan, Amy took the Bible and papers. She said she would hide them. I told her that if she is caught, they would do terrible things to her.

"What? Are you crazy? Why would you let her take them?"

Ryan was furious for so many reasons, most of them protective reasons. He cared about Amy and didn't want to think of how they would torture her to get any information. There would be no sleeping now. He started planning on how to get Amy to give him the papers so that if anyone got caught and tortured, it would be him. Now all he had to do was convince her that it was the right thing to do. He told Bill his plan.

"I argued the same reasoning with Amy, but got nowhere. All I can say is 'Be careful.'" Bill rolled back over on his side and went to sleep.

Ryan watched Amy sleep. He prayed over her and asked God to protect her. As soon as Amy opened her eyes, she saw Ryan's gaze on her.

"Ryan, you okay?" Her voice was soft as the presence of sleep was still upon her.

"I know what you have and I want them so I can hide them. I don't want you in such danger. Tell me where they are and I will take care of them." Ryan expected her to agree and do what he asked. He sure got a surprise.

"I will not!" All the sleepiness in her voice had jumped overboard! She was firm, direct, and unstoppable. It's taken care of and too dangerous to move now.

It didn't take a rocket scientist to figure out that Amy wasn't budging. Ryan didn't try to argue. He actually liked her spunk. Her outgoingness complimented his quiet nature. Her determination and his strength were a good match. They docked for the last time and taxied to the airport. Amy refused to tell any of them where the Bible pages were. She felt it was safer that way.

Every fear and dread they felt coming into the country was multiplied by thousands. They no sooner got into customs that they were being pulled aside and searched. Every inch of their bodies was touched. All their suitcases and luggage was opened up and searched. Amy had her hair pulled up in a bun and they made her pull it down. The bongo cases were opened and searched. Bill was so thankful that God had given him the dream. God was watching out for them. Amy was held back and searched without mercy. Her personal items were dumped out for everyone to view. The white and black stones that she had collected on the beach were spilled out and they fell to the floor. Amy bent over and picked up the stones that were representative of her memories and put them back in her bag.

"What you have?" The guard spoke to Amy in a hateful tone.

"I don't know what you are asking." Amy remained so calm. She was in total peace as the guard touched her and humiliated her in front of the others.

"You have words for me?" The guard was looking for any type of behavior or excuse to hold Amy from the others. They threw Amy's belongings on the floor like trash, including the beautiful Mat that Razan had made her. The guards walked back and forth on her clothes before they finally gave her permission to pick up her things. Finally, unable to get a reaction out of any of them, they released them to go. With only minutes to catch their plane, they ran the full length of the airport, barely making last boarding call.

It wasn't until they had all been seated and the plane started rolling down the runway that they felt safe. Amy had an emotional meltdown. She didn't mean to, but couldn't help herself. She had been so strong as the guards patted her down and bullied her. Now, her hands started shaking, then her whole body. She became cold all over and her face flushed red hot. If she didn't find a form of relief, she was going to explode.

Ryan sat next to Amy. He was so aware of her. He could literally see her temperature rise in her cheeks. He didn't ask permission. He didn't care what others thought. As soon as the sign flashed that it was safe to remove his seatbelt, Ryan unfastened his belt and put his right arm firmly around her. She buried her face in his shoulder and cried. She cried long and hard. Ryan held her, not expecting conversation or apologies. The stewardess came by once to hand them tissues. When Amy finally stopped crying, Ryan looked down at her and she was sound asleep.

They landed in London for another four-hour layover. Ryan gently nudged Amy awake. His right arm had been asleep almost as long as Amy, but he was afraid to move, fearing he would wake her. His arm tingled and burned when Amy sat up and he moved his arm.

"I can't believe I slept all the way to London!" Amy stretched and yawn trying to get revived.

"You slept through the refueling too." Ryan informed her as he watched her move around.

Amy felt the warmth rising in her cheeks again, but this time it was because she saw Ryan looking at her. "I must look dreadful." She rubbed her face and pulled her hair back.

"No Amy, not even close." Ryan picked up the used tissues that had fallen to the floor while she was crying earlier. "Come on. We are the last ones on the plane." He reached for her elbow to help her up, but Amy reached out her hand instead.

"Thank you, Ryan." She showed her sincerity by looking at him and not breaking her gaze until he accepted her appreciation.

"You are welcome. Let's go." If the aisle way had not been so narrow, Ryan probably would not have let go of her hand.

"I thought you two were lost in there," Mark said as they finally got off the plane. Amy didn't banter with him this time. Mark was rather disappointed. He had gotten use to Amy always having a comeback and putting him in his place.

"Where is the nearest coffee shop? Caffeine is calling my name." Wayne led the way because he wanted coffee and wanted it now!

Civilization, coffee, and junk food made for some happy Americans. They found a table with enough seating for all of them. "Amy you did a great job at the Maldives airport." Bill spoke first and then all the men agreed with him.

"Where are the papers? Where did you hide them?" With caffeine finally in his system, Wayne was ready for conversation.

Amy looked at Bill for confirmation that it was safe to tell before she spoke. "I would like to know too," Bill added.

"I did horrible at rope-making, but I turned out to be a really good mat-weaver. I had made a mat myself and Razan gave me one the night before we left. I laid all the papers out on Razan's mat and carefully wove my mat to hers. I knew it had to be a tight weave in order to keep the papers safe. I was up all night weaving and praying." Amy revealed a big part of her exhaustion. Everyone but her slept that night. She had the mat with her. She took it out of her carry-on and handed it to him. "The papers are weaved in the mat. If you please, be careful when you take the papers out. This mat means a lot to me.

"Wow! Smart thinking," Bill admitted that he never came up with a safe way to smuggle out the papers. "God gave you a great answer. Almost all visitors take mats home with them as souvenirs. They would not have thought to tear apart your mat. And of course," he added. "I will take great care of your mat."

They chatted and went over the past four weeks. They talked and laughed at their experiences. It was good. It was really good.

"Our dad was right," Wayne admitted. "One mission trip and your life will never be the same."

Chapter Fourteen

Amy - The Brave

The rest of the journey was, thankfully, uneventful. Ryan and Bill threw different scenarios around about how to get the Bibles printed and smuggled back into Maldives. All their suggestions, when thought out, had road blocks.

"God will work things out," Bill finally concluded. "This is bigger than our brains right now. When we put things into perspective, we must know that God loves them more than we do. He wants us to succeed, therefore we will. We don't have to have it all figured out. That's God's job."

Ryan thought about Bill's words. They were true, but his burning desire to help the Maldives people know God would sometimes be getting his cart before God's horse. Backing off wasn't easy. Then there was Amy. He wasn't ready or willing to let her go either. He had never had a girlfriend and yet he knew who he wanted as a wife… Amy.

The landing in Cincinnati was smooth. They were officially home. The brother's father was waiting for them. When the brothers saw their father, they ran to him. As if they were little boys again, they dropped their carry-on luggage and hugged their father. He looked so proud of his sons.

Amy's mom, dad, and sister waited patiently for their daughter to appear out of the tunnel. As soon as her brothers heard their mom squeal in excitement, her brothers stopped chasing each other around and ran to join in on the family group hug. Ryan watched. He was thankful that Amy had people to love her so much. He was sure that was the reason why she was able to love so freely and talk to anyone. All that was left were Bill and Ryan.

"Over here," came a voice behind a large group of people. It was Bill's associate. "Sorry, traffic was horrible," he complained.

"Ryan, Ryan Nelson? Is there a Ryan Nelson here?" It was the airport attendant. "I have a message for Mr. Ryan Nelson."

"That's me," Ryan said. The attendant handed him a note. It was from Ed. He was apologizing for not being able to pick him up at the airport. He had a family emergency and could not pick him up for four more hours. Everyone was looking at him. "I'm fine. You all go on. Please keep in touch." He wanted them to leave quickly. He was reminded once again that his family was... different. He had food and a roof over his head growing up, but no family. Ed was wonderful. He and his family had demonstrated what a true family was supposed to be like. He knew that if Ed could be there, he would have been.

Not one of his mission friends moved. They were not going to leave him at the airport. As much as they wanted to go back to their homes and tell everyone their experiences, they didn't want to leave Ryan. They all had grown that close.

"We live close, Ryan. You can come with us and call your friend when we get to the house. He can pick you up there." It was Mr. Waltz speaking.

"Thank you sir, but I will be fine here," Ryan replied.

Amy's dad didn't budge. "Nonsense young man, you will

come home with us." His voice was sincere and firm. Ryan thought of it as a nice demand.

"Yes Sir," Ryan replied this time. Handshakes and hugs sent everyone on their way and Ryan with Amy's family.

Ryan sat in the back of the station wagon and listened to all the commotion going on around him. Amy's large family was a little intimidating to him. Amy shared the highlights and then answered fifty questions. Ryan didn't engage in any conversation, even when Amy mentioned his name. This was her time to share and shine. She was exceptional and brave. He watched her glow as she talked about the children she played with in Fuvahmulah. He cringed as she told them of how hard the coir rope was and how it cut her hand. He remembered the cut too. It was the second time he had touched her hand. Then, for the first and only time, he heard her brag.

"I became great at mat weaving. It was like it came so natural to me," Amy said. Although she didn't have proof of her talents now, she would one day.

They pulled up into the driveway of a nice two-story house with a large detached garage. Ryan looked all around. He was so in tune to Amy that he hadn't been paying attention to where they were. There were no neighbors anywhere. "They must have ten acres here," Ryan thought to himself. The house and land was beautiful.

Amy's siblings had heard enough. As soon as the car stopped, they jumped out of the car and took off. Mr. and Mrs. Waltz helped to unload the car and they all went inside. Mr. Waltz showed Ryan where the phone was so he could call Ed. Ed's mom was the one who answered. It turned out that Carol had been sick. What they were blaming on the flu turned out to be a bad appendix. She had received emergency surgery that morning. Ed's mom was staying with the older girls while Ed and Nancy stayed at the hospital with Carol. It might be a few days before Ed could come and get him. Ryan left the number to the Waltz's home and asked that Ed call him when he was able.

"I would take you back myself, Ryan, but I am so backed up here at work, that taking half a day off might bury me for a week." Mr. Waltz was kind to offer, but Ryan would not have accepted anyway.

"I am sorry, Mr. Waltz. I don't want to burden you here. Um, I am not sure what to do right now." Ryan hated being in this position. Even if it meant being close to Amy.

Mr. Waltz felt for the young man. There had to be a reason why his family didn't come to get him. He would get details from Amy later. Right now, the young man needed a place to stay. "I have a small apartment in the top of the garage. The roof is gable styled, so across the middle 15 feet or so is the only part where you can stand up straight. It has a couch that folds out into a bed, a bathroom with a shower stall and a kitchenette. It's not fancy or homey, but you will have your needs met."

"Are you sure, Sir? I can go somewhere…" Ryan was interrupted by "No." Mr. Waltz didn't play with words. Ryan had a place to stay.

"After dinner, I will show you around." Mr. Waltz led the way to the kitchen where everyone was scrambling around for a seat. Mrs. Waltz had put a roast with potatoes, celery, and carrots in the oven before they left for the airport. The whole house smelled delicious.

The Waltz household reminded Ryan of Ed's house. They thanked God for the food before they ate. They had conversations involving everyone and they included Ryan in on their chaos. It was fun. Ryan enjoyed every bite of food and every minute of conversation.

After dinner, Mr. Waltz took Ryan out to the garage. It was dark by this time. He unlocked the door and ran his hand along the inside wall searching for the light switch. "There it is." He flipped the switch and they walked in.

Ryan was shocked as he looked around. This was no ordinary garage. A small factory would be a better description. It had been expanded at least once from what Ryan could tell. He estimated the building to be 200 feet long and 60 feet wide. "What in the world is that machine?! What are all those boxes for? Look at that pile of cardboard. Why do you have all those shelves?" Ryan didn't stop there. He had a thousand questions.

"Hold on, young man. Slow down, one question at a time. Or better yet, let me talk and then if you have questions, you can ask." Mr. Waltz started from the beginning.

CHAPTER FIFTEEN

REVEALING DIRECTION

Ryan could feel a bubbling in his stomach and it wasn't his food digesting. Something big was about to be revealed.

"I run a small packaging company out of here," Mr. Waltz explained. "I have worked out of my garage for years. I've never had any problems getting orders out until this summer. I bought this here machine in March, about the same time Amy wanted to go to Maldives. That's why she had to make a choice to go out of state to college or go on the mission trip. This machine cost a bundle."

He walked Ryan over to a large machine sitting in the middle of his garage. In bold print the word EMBEA was stamped on its side. Mr. Waltz explained the whole process of the "big boss" as he called it. "This machine can be programmed to slot, slit, and crease a box any way you please. I can box up and send a coffee mug or a refrigerator clear across the states," he said proudly with a big smile on his face. "It will even glue the folds," he exclaimed.

The problem is I have so much inventory now that I have outgrown the place. Mrs. Waltz refuses to let me add another inch to the garage. She says if it were up to me the whole yard would be a factory." Mr. Waltz was making jokes, but Ryan was as serious as a heart attack.

"Do you think you could ever export anything with this machine?" Ryan's question wasn't an 'in theory' question. The wheels in his head were turning and his blood was pumping strong. With a five minute conversation in the garage, Ryan had a vision on how to get the Bibles to Maldives.

"All it takes is a product and a contract!" Mr. Waltz was so confident in his EMBEA. Little did he know that all his confidence was soon to be put to the test. "Sounds like you have something in mind, Ryan."

"I do Sir, Bibles and to be more specific, Bibles to Maldives." Ryan didn't crack a smile when he spoke. Now Mr. Waltz knew he was being challenged.

"You have no idea what you are asking. There has to be merchandise going that direction first. We have to bid on contracts, win the bid, sign legal papers with both our government and the country to which the product is going." He went on and on with details before asking, "Are you overwhelmed by this information yet?" Mr. Waltz had only just met Ryan. He had no idea of Ryan's determination.

"No, not even close, Sir," now Ryan smiled.

"Look around you. I don't have room for anything else in this garage. I am working day and night to stay true to the people I package for already. I went out last week and looked at warehouses around the city. The prices for rent are more than I make in a month. I can tell that you and Amy were strongly impacted by your trip, but there are desires and then there is reality. I am a man of great faith in God. I have seen Him work more miracles in my lifetime than ten men put together. I am sorry, Ryan. Don't make plans for this to happen." A knock at the door was all Mr. Waltz needed to escape from Ryan's big dream.

"Hi Daddy, Ryan, What are you two doing out here?"

Amy could feel tenseness in the atmosphere.

"Ryan is going to be staying up in the garage apartment until he can make it back home." Mr. Waltz excused himself and left Amy and Ryan standing in the garage.

Ryan explained why Amy felt the way she did. She was sensitive to situations and picked up emotions easily. Amy finished walking Ryan around the garage and shared everything she knew about her father's work, albeit not much. She walked him up the stairs and opened the door. She turned on the lights and showed him around, which took about thirty seconds. The kitchen area was the first room inside the door. There wasn't enough room for a table, so a snack bar was built out from the wall as part of the cabinet. There were two bar stools pushed under the cabinet. Ryan pulled them both out and asked Amy to sit with him.

"Amy, can you see this packaging company being a key to smuggling Bibles? Can you see how this can become a reality?" Ryan wanted her to say "yes" badly. He wanted to share this and so much more with her.

"Yes, I do. However, it isn't me that you have to convince, it's my father." Amy weighed and measured her words carefully. She had the same passion for Maldives that Ryan did. She did not want to sound like she was defending her dad. Finally, she spoke with a clear understanding of both sides of the situation. "My dad is a good man. He works hard and gives easily. He is very proud of that new machine downstairs. He never intended for anyone to know this, but he borrowed against the house to buy that big beast. Mom told me because she thought I would be disappointed in not being able to go to Maldives and go to college out of state." Amy twisted on the bar stool to reposition herself and think.

Ryan waited on Amy to finish. He wanted to hear everything so he would know how to pray. "I don't want to hurt your feelings, Ryan. I am going to ask you to think about what you said to my dad and then add the information I just gave you. In the past four weeks, we have had our eyes opened to a great need. We are anxious to help those beautiful people. However, in order to do so, we need the help of my dad who has put his home up for collateral in order for his business to grow. It is a big risk for him to take."

Ryan was quiet. He began to realize that he had pushed his vision on Mr. Waltz unfairly. "I'm sorry, Amy. I didn't know all the circumstances. Will you please pray with me?"

Amy didn't hesitate. They prayed, then and there, God's will be done.

"I need to speak with your father, Amy. I have to talk to him. It's important." Ryan sounded as if he were begging. Maybe he was in a way.

"You have given Dad a lot to think about. Let him sleep on it tonight. He will be up making plenty of noise in here very early. You better get sleep while you can." Amy got up from the stool and started to walk away. As she turned, Ryan reached once again for her hand.

"May I hug you Amy?" It was sweet, it was innocent, and it was a proclamation by Ryan.

Amy didn't answer. She positioned herself in front of him. He took a small step forward and put his arms gently around her. He hugged her briefly and raised his hands up to her face. He looked at her. For the first time he saw how beautiful she was physically. For four weeks he had repeatedly seen the beauty of her heart. Yes, he had noticed her looks before, but not like this.

Amy's breathing was shallow. She wanted him to kiss her. It would be a first kiss for them both, but tonight wasn't perfect enough for Ryan.

"Goodnight, Amy. I will see you tomorrow." He released her face and stepped back.

Amy floated down the stairs and into the house. She was

feeling very blessed.

At 6:30 in the morning, Ryan was awakened by a deep humming sound coming from the garage below. He felt like he hadn't slept at all. He stumbled to the small restroom to wash the sleep out of his eyes. The restroom was so small that he was practically standing in the shower as he washed his face. He decided that a shower would help him more. After he was showered and shaved, he dressed for the day. He felt great now. It may be a small restroom, but it had great water pressure.

As Ryan came down the stairs, he could see Mr. Waltz at the EMBEA hard at work. "Morning, Ryan," he called out to Ryan when he spotted him across the room.

"Morning, sir," Ryan had a desire to learn everything about this process. He had a plan and a prayer. "Can I help you this morning?"

"Sure, see those flat sheets of cardboard over there? Go pick up ten sheets. There is a conveyer belt to Big Boss down on that far side. I'm finishing up these calibrations here and then we will make some boxes." Mr. Waltz added more to the final touches and measurements. "You have them loaded?"

"Yes, Sir," Ryan answered.

"Keep your hands back," he warned. "This machine will either tear your arm off or flatten you like a pancake. You have to respect Big Boss." Mr. Waltz's name for the EMBEA machine reminded him of Ed and how he named his cars. "Here we go."

The ten flat boxes were pulled into the machine all at once. Ryan walked over to Mr. Waltz as he explained what was going on inside the machine. "It's corrugating now. The next step will put it through a rotary die cutter. Those blades are so sharp that they can go through the whole stack of cardboard at once. Look, look there. You see that part of the machine?" He was pointing proudly at something. Ryan couldn't tell what it was that was pointing to. To Ryan, the whole thing was awesome.

"That is the printer/slotter. It takes the boxes already cut to size and cuts the slots out for the ends so they can be folded and glued. The last step is that part right there." There he went pointing again. Ryan was clueless, but nodded yes anyway.

"That is the last thing this machine does. It will print logos on the boxes. Pretty impressive isn't it?" Mr. Waltz loved his new toy.

"Very, very impressive," Ryan replied. Ryan helped him load cardboard, package inventory and stack the finished products.

"Daddy," Amy called. You have a phone call." Mr. Waltz looked at his watch. It was 10:30 already. Ryan had been such a big help that the morning flew by.

"Coming, Honey," he yelled back to Amy. "Have you eaten anything?" Ryan shook his head no.

"I am a hard worker, but not a slave driver. Have Amy get you something to eat while I get the phone."

Amy fixed Ryan some eggs and toast. They stayed in the kitchen for a half an hour talking about everything except the last five minutes of last evening. Ryan stood beside Amy drying the dishes as she washed them. Mr. Waltz finished his phone call and asked Ryan if he was ready to get back to work.

They went back to the garage and started working even harder than before. Mr. Waltz's disposition had changed. Something happened during the phone call, but Ryan never questioned him. Four hours later, Amy came to tell her dad that he had yet another phone call. It was 3:00 in the afternoon and the ladies of the family already had the house smelling like a restaurant. Ryan's brunch had worn off three hours ago and the aroma of the house started his stomach complaining. Amy laughed when she heard his stomach roar in protest.

"Are you going to live until dinner?" Amy teased.

"Depends on how long I have to wait," Ryan said grabbing his mid-section in dramatic fashion. "I may vanish away."

Amy laughed at him and offered him some cookies and milk to tie him over. "Oh yes, COOKIES! That is a way to my heart for sure." Ryan had just embarrassed himself. He couldn't believe those words came from his mouth.

"Well then, I better see what we have," Amy bantered back. She pulled down two cups and found half dozen cookies which was a miracle in itself, considering how many kids there were running around the house. They were comfortable with each other. They felt a mutual acceptance and pleasure in each other's company.

Mr. Waltz came into the kitchen with the same look on his face that he had from his last phone call. This couldn't be good. "Amy, tell your mom we are ready for dinner as soon as it's ready. Ryan, I need to see you out in the garage." With those words spoken, he turned and walked away expecting Ryan to be right behind him. He was.

"Are you okay, Mr. Waltz?" Ryan was concerned.

"You better explain to me exactly how you are praying." Mr. Waltz wiped his face with his handkerchief. Those two phone calls were unexplainable and unexpected. I didn't sleep hardly at all last night. Every time I closed my eyes, I saw my daughter beaming as she talked about the children of Maldives she fell in love with. Then at some point you would appear in my dream with your idea to use my business to smuggle Bibles."

Mr. Waltz leaned against Big Boss and wiped his face once again. He was sweating and it wasn't hot in the garage. "You aren't going to believe this. This morning, the first phone call was from the owner of an empty manufactory building. I toured that building last week and felt so strong to put in a bid to buy the property and the building. The number in my head was $100,000.00 less than the asking price. The realtor was hateful with me. She thought I was wasting everyone's time and wasn't shy to let me know it, too. There was a twenty-four-hour reply to my offer in the contract and I never heard back from the realtor, until this morning. The owner wants to get rid of the property. He said he would give it to me at my price as long as I agree to clean it out."

Ryan's concern turned straight to delight. The look on Ryan's face said, yes, I can believe it. We are talking about God's miracles!

"And then…," Mr. Waltz continued. "I just hung up from a guy in Kentucky who wants to ship his product to Canada. This is a huge contract and what makes it better is that it is an ongoing need, not a one-time thing. The money from that contract alone will pay for the factory. This is bigger than me at this point."

"Not bigger than God." Ryan was trying not to be smug about Mr. Waltz's new revelation because it was his vision first. He didn't know exactly how God was going to get His plan in action, but Ryan knew He would complete the task.

"Ryan is there anything else I need to know now. I am totally in awe of God's work at this point. Are there going to be other surprises ahead that I should prepare myself for? You seem to have an insight to all this so I thought I should ask." Mr. Waltz was very serious and so was Ryan.

"Yes Sir, there is one more thing." Ryan straightened his posture and looked him in the eyes. "I love your daughter and I want to marry her…"

Also available:

QUIET STRENGTH BOOK SERIES

BOOK II
THE OFFERING

BOOK III
ELI'S JOURNEY

ABOUT THE AUTHOR

Tina was born and raised in Southwest Ohio. She has four main passions in her life; her faith, family, writing and Cincinnati Reds Baseball. With a blended family of six children and four grandchildren, Tina lives and writes with a passion to see young adults overcoming obstacles, coming into their own, and finding God's will for their lives.

OTHER BOOKS BY TINA:

QUIET STRENGTH BOOK II-THE OFFERING

What starts as a mission of love becomes so much more after Ryan and Amy met on a trip to the beautiful coral island country of Maldives. A passion for translating God's word into the Dhivehi language is the first step of many to get the truth of God's word into a country that proclaims to be 100% Muslim. When the gospel of Luke is finally translated, the bigger problem becomes how to get the illegal material into Maldives. God opens eyes and opens doors for the young couple to smuggle the gospel.

Ryan and Amy devote their love to each other and their lives to Christ in the face of danger and death. With Ryan's vow to Amy to never leave her behind, the couple embarks on a journey to get God's word into the hands of those who hunger for its truth and peace.

IN SELF-DEFENSE
(eBook)

Randi knows what she wants and needs to survive. Smothered by a dominating mother and supposed fiancé, her attempts for independence are half-hearted, but completely ignored. After a frightful and threatening experience, Randi has a decision to make; does she return home to her mother's 'I told you so…', does she marry her fiancé and be taken care of for the rest of her life, or does the desire and determination to be free from dominance finally force her to take a stand? In her own self-defense, can she win the respect of her mom and the fight for both her heart and life?

98

WHEN GOD SAID NO
(eBook)

When God Said No is the true story of one woman's faith during her battle with cancer and the trust and faith she instills in the heart of a child. Dawn is in remission when she starts babysitting the six-week-old, Ava. Over the next five years, a bond develops between them that circumstances cannot break apart. Dawn's unwavering trust in God, humor and determination to live in faith, inspires everyone. The faith of a child inspires Dawn.

Subscribe to my blog:
tinahawkeybaker.wordpress.com

If you enjoyed this book, please remember to leave a review at your favorite retailer. Thank you for your support.

Made in the USA
Monee, IL
05 July 2020

35876134R00066